WHEN the CURTAIN RISES

WHEN the CURTAIN RISES

Rachel Dunstan Muller

Orca Book Publishers

Library and Archives Canada Cataloguing in Publication

Muller, Rachel Dunstan, 1970-
When the curtain rises / written by Rachel Dunstan Muller.

ISBN-13: 978-1-55143-615-9
ISBN-10: 1-55143-615-9

I. Title.

PS8626.U445W44 2007   jC813'.6   C2006-906136-X

First published in the United States, 2007
Library of Congress Control Number: 2006937244

Summary: Chloe confronts her own fears when she investigates the strange history of her great-grandfather, a magician who disappeared at the height of his popularity.

Orca Book Publishers gratefully acknowledges the support for its publishing programs provided by the following agencies: the Government of Canada through the Book Publishing Industry Development Program and the Canada Council for the Arts, and the Province of British Columbia through the BC Arts Council and the Book Publishing Tax Credit.

Typesetting by Christine Toller
Cover artwork by Pol Turgen

Orca Book Publishers
PO Box 5626, Stn. B
Victoria, BC Canada
V8R 6S4

Orca Book Publishers
PO Box 468
Custer, WA USA
98240-0468

www.orcabook.com
Printed and bound in Canada.
Printed on 100% PCW paper.

10 09 08 07 • 4 3 2 1

For Bern, who believed.

Chapter One

"I had the weirdest dream last night," Chloe said as she slid into her seat at the kitchen table.

Her father looked up from his crossword puzzle. "Another nightmare?"

Chloe shook her head. "Not exactly."

"You're up early on your first day of vacation," said her mother. She pushed a box of cornflakes in Chloe's direction.

"I've been awake since six. I couldn't get back to sleep."

"So what was so strange about your dream?" asked her father.

Chloe shrugged, pushing aside a curl that had fallen into her eyes. "I don't know. It just felt so *real*. Like I was *there*. I was walking down a street through an old-fashioned town. On one side of the street there was a river, almost like a canal. The other side of the street was lined with tall houses. I stopped in front of the biggest one and just stood there staring at it. It was familiar somehow. Then I heard a woman call my name. I couldn't see who it was, but when I woke up I could still hear her voice in my head. It gave me goose bumps."

Chloe's parents exchanged glances. "It sounds like the house in Little Venice," said her father.

"What house?" Chloe said.

"Don't you remember?" asked her father.

"It's been about ten years since our last visit, Sam," Chloe's mother pointed out. "Chloe couldn't have been more than two or three."

"You're right," said her father. "The old ladies couldn't get enough of you, Chloe, as I recall. The three of you were inseparable the entire time we were there."

"What old ladies?" Chloe asked. "I don't know what you're talking about."

"Maybe this will refresh your memory," said her mother. She held up a cream envelope. "This came for you yesterday. I found it when I was sorting through the bills this morning."

Chloe took the heavy envelope from her mother's manicured hand. There was no return address, but the envelope was postmarked Little Venice, Ontario. She broke the seal with her thumbnail. As she was removing the single folded page, a tiny golden key dropped into her lap. She picked up the key and stared at it for a moment before putting it on the table and turning her attention to the letter. She read the short note twice. There was no mention of the tiny key.

"Well, what does it say?" asked her father.

"It's an invitation," said Chloe, slightly bewildered. "From your aunts, Dad. Elizabeth and Katherine. They want me to spend the summer with them in Little Venice."

"Really?" said her mother. "How nice."

"I'm not going," Chloe said as she shoved the folded note back into its envelope. "It would be too weird."

"What would be weird about it?" her father asked. "You could use a distraction right now. A change of scenery."

"Dad," Chloe said, turning red. "Don't start."

"Start what? I'm not starting anything. I just said you could use a vacation."

"Mom!"

"Don't look at me," said her mother, raising her hands. "I think spending some time in Little Venice this summer is a great idea."

Chloe eyed her parents suspiciously. "You knew about this before I even opened the letter, didn't you?"

"Yes, we did," her mother admitted. "Your great-aunts called us a few weeks ago. They haven't seen you for a long time, and your dad and I talked about it and agreed that the timing was perfect. Your father's right, Chloe. A vacation would be a really healthy thing for you right now."

"So let's all go to Hawaii, then."

"You know I can't get away from Edmonton this summer," said her mother. "With Jacqueline on maternity leave, my caseload has exploded. I'm lucky if I get to go to the bathroom these days."

"We could always enroll you in summer camp some-where," her father said.

Chloe shook her head in alarm. "No way!"

"Right," said her father. "Then why not give your great-aunts a try?"

"But I don't even *know* them! A visit when I was in diapers hardly counts."

Chloe's mother put her empty bowl down on the counter and picked up her briefcase. "Here's your chance, then. Your great-aunts are getting old. They won't be around forever."

"Do I have a choice?" asked Chloe.

Her father shrugged. "Of course you have a choice, Chloe. But think about it. You don't have to go for the whole summer— how about just for a month? Little Venice is a magical place. I used to spend my vacations there, and I loved it."

Chloe waited until both her parents were gone—her mother to her law office and her father to his music store in the mall—before getting up from the table. She cleaned up the kitchen, started the dishwasher and went directly to the baby grand piano in the living room.

Chloe lifted the heavy lid and ran her fingertips lightly over the keys. "Here goes nothing," she told herself with a sigh, flexing her fingers. She moved quickly through her scales and then played a few practice pieces from memory. When she was satisfied that her hands were warmed up, she arranged the sheet music for Chopin's Nocturne in F-sharp Major on the narrow shelf in front of her. She took a few deep breaths and began.

Everything was fine as long as Chloe kept her mind empty of everything but the music. But as soon as she let the image of an audience creep into her mind, her pulse began to race and her hands started to tremble.

Chloe took a few calming breaths and started over again. This time she visualized Mrs. Jann, her piano teacher, seated on a stool beside her. But even that simple image distracted Chloe and made her stumble as she played.

"This is *stupid*!" Chloe cried after several more failed attempts to play the piece through to its conclusion. She let her clenched hands fall into her lap. Her head fell forward against the music on the ledge. "I can't do this," she whispered. "It's too hard."

"So. What did you do today?" her father asked as he tossed diced vegetables and pieces of chicken in a sizzling wok that evening.

"Not much," Chloe said. "Ashley came over for a while. Her family's driving up to Yellowknife next week to visit her brother."

"How long is she going to be gone?"

Chloe frowned. "A whole month. They're going camping all over the place."

"It'll be boring here for you without Ashley around. Did you give any more thought to your great-aunts' invitation?"

"I wouldn't exactly call spending my vacation with two ninety-year-olds an 'exciting' alternative," said Chloe.

"Don't write them off just because of their age," said her father. "Your old aunts have a lot of life left in them. They might surprise you."

Chloe was silent for a moment as she fingered the tiny

key that still sat where she'd left it on the table. "So, what do you think this key is for, anyway?" she asked.

Her father reached for the tiny key and weighed it in his hand. "It's too small to be a room key. Maybe it unlocks a small chest or a jewelry box or the lock on a journal. But who knows? Your great-aunts' house is full of mysteries."

"Like what?"

"Like hidden rooms and secret passageways, for starters."

"Really?" Chloe said, her eyebrows rising.

"Really," her father replied with a grin. "Curious yet?"

Chloe felt the corners of her own mouth curl up slightly. "Maybe. Just a little."

A week later, Chloe rose early and followed her parents out to the driveway. As she waited for her father to finish loading her luggage into the trunk of her mother's Audi, Chloe fingered the tiny golden key that she'd hung on a chain around her neck. She continued playing with it absently all the way to the airport.

Chloe's parents stayed with her while she checked her luggage and picked up her boarding pass. At the final security checkpoint, they said their goodbyes.

"Now don't forget. Your great-aunts' housekeeper, Abigail, will be waiting for you in Toronto," said Chloe's father. "She'll have a sign with your name on it, so you won't be able to miss her."

Chloe nodded, trying to hide her impatience. "I remember. I'll be fine, don't worry."

"Use your calling card to call us when you get in," said her mother.

"I will."

"And give the old girls a hug for me," said her father. "By the way," he added, "I believe your great-aunts still have an old upright piano tucked away somewhere. Just in case you get the urge to play a few scales."

"Sam!" said Chloe's mother, shaking her head sternly. "Give her a break!" She took her daughter's hand. "Your counselor said you need some time off. Even Mrs. Jann agreed."

"I've got to go," said Chloe, tugging her hand away. "They're calling my flight."

"I love you, Chloe," said her mother.

"Me too," said her father.

"I love you too." Chloe kissed her parents goodbye and broke away to join the line that led through the security checkpoint. She turned to wave at them one last time when she was on the other side of the metal detectors.

As she made her way to her departure gate, Chloe felt an unexpected rush of exhilaration sweep through her body. She was on her own, setting off on an adventure halfway across the country.

A stout woman with graying brown hair was waiting in the arrivals area at the Toronto airport, holding up a small handwritten sign that said *Chloe McBride*. The woman's eyes lit up behind her wire-rimmed glasses when she saw Chloe approaching.

"Chloe! You look just like your school pictures. I'm Abigail. I can't tell you how thrilled your aunts are that you're coming. Kitty's been counting down the days like a schoolgirl!"

The housekeeper's good humor was hard to resist. Chloe smiled back.

"Let me carry that for you," said Abigail, reaching for Chloe's carry-on bag. Chloe started to protest, but the bag had already been snatched away. "Now let's track down the rest of your luggage—assuming the airline hasn't sent it to Paraguay."

Abigail continued to chatter as she led Chloe to her tiny hatchback, parked in the bowels of the airport parkade. By the time they'd stopped for burgers and fries just off the freeway near London, Chloe had only managed to insert about a dozen words into the conversation.

It was almost eight o'clock when they finally reached the turnoff for Little Venice. As the hatchback left the highway and drove through the outskirts of the small town, Chloe felt goose bumps rise on her arms. The view outside her window was ordinary enough. Tall maples, oaks and chestnut trees formed shady tunnels along residential streets. Children played on trim front lawns and rode bikes and scooters up and down the wide sidewalks. It could have been an older neighborhood in almost any city, but somehow, even though Chloe had no memory of ever being here, it seemed strangely familiar.

The car turned and turned again, and they made their way through the center of town. Pretty, old-fashioned storefronts painted in bright colors lined the town's streets. Pedestrians spilled over the brick sidewalks.

"Everyone wants to be in Little Venice in the summertime," Abigail said. "It's a magical town—there's no other place quite like it."

Chloe nodded, drinking it all in. "My father called it that too. Magical."

They drove over a long stone bridge that crossed a canal. "The Grand Canal," said Abigail. "Little Venice was modeled after the original Venice in Italy. The town founders carved out the first canal, but they never got around to all the lesser ones. Cost too much, I guess. This one starts down at the lake and ends at St. Mark's Theatre." She gestured toward a large domed building at the far end of the canal. "We're almost home now."

Chloe drew in her breath. With a ribbon of shining water on one side of the street and a row of proud Victorian mansions on the other, it was almost as if Abigail were driving her through the setting of the dream she'd had the night before she received her invitation. As Chloe released her breath, Abigail pulled over to the curb and parked.

"This is it," the housekeeper announced.

It was all just as she remembered from her dream: the wraparound veranda, the overflowing window boxes at the lower windows, the turrets and balconies and widow's walk above. But Chloe only had a moment to take in the house before two tiny elderly women appeared on the front steps.

"Chloe!" one of them called out, clapping in delight. "You made it!"

"I told you," said Abigail. She nudged Chloe forward. "Kitty's been positively beside herself."

Chloe was gathered into a soft lavender-scented hug the moment she reached the steps of the veranda. "Welcome to Little Venice, my dear," said the old woman in whose slender arms Chloe was wrapped. "We're so happy you decided to come!"

"You're going to smother her, Kitty," said the second old woman. "Well, let's have a look at you," she continued. Her green eyes scanned Chloe's face. "You've got your mother's mouth, but there's still something of the McBrides up around your eyes."

"And that hair," said the first woman, reaching out to touch Chloe's brown curls.

The second woman nodded. "She definitely has Magdala's hair."

"Oh, Bess!" The first old woman raised her hand to her mouth. "Where are our manners? We've been chattering like magpies without introducing ourselves. I'm Kitty and she's Bess," she said to Chloe. "We're identical twins, but you shouldn't have too much trouble telling us apart. I'll give you a hint," she added in a stage whisper. "I like wearing violet, and Bess favors blue."

"Only one of us is chattering," Bess remarked. She turned to Chloe. "Put that bag down and come have a seat on the veranda. I don't imagine you've had any decent food since you left home this morning."

"I'm fine," Chloe protested. "We stopped for burgers and fries on our way from the airport."

Bess waved her hands in the air dismissively. "That's not real food."

"We have strawberry shortcake," said Kitty. "You don't want to pass up our shortcake, my dear. Abigail picked the strawberries and I whipped the cream myself," she continued, steering Chloe toward a wicker chair on the veranda.

Abigail stepped inside the house and returned a moment later with a tray. "Don't worry," the housekeeper whispered as she handed Chloe her shortcake and a tall glass of iced tea. "You'll get a chance to catch your breath eventually."

Chapter Two

Chloe had intended to get up early the next morning, but the clock on the bedside table said eight thirty when the knock on her door woke her up. "Wha'? Hello?" she said, momentarily disoriented.

"It's just me." Abigail's voice came from the hallway. "I'm about to put breakfast on the table."

"Thanks," Chloe mumbled. She pushed herself out of bed, slipped on her bathrobe and followed her nose out to the kitchen.

"Did you sleep well?" Abigail asked as she removed two waffles from a waffle iron. Bacon and eggs sizzled behind her in a pan on the stove.

Chloe yawned and nodded. "That's the softest bed I've ever slept in. It was like sleeping on a cloud."

"You can thank your great-aunts for that. They like everyone to be very comfortable," said Abigail. "Speaking of your aunts, they're just through here having their morning tea. Be a dear and hold the door while I carry in this tray."

"Good morning, Chloe," Kitty said as Chloe entered the dining room behind the housekeeper.

Bess nodded from her place on the other side of the oval table.

"How did you sleep? Is your room all right?" asked Kitty. "It used to be a larder, but we had it converted into a bedroom years ago, for when your father visited. We liked to keep him on the same floor with us when he was small. Our bedrooms are just down the hall. But you're not a little girl—we could give you a room on one of the upper floors if you'd prefer more space or privacy."

"I slept well. I like the room," Chloe said as she spread her napkin across her lap. "It's cozy. And the view into the garden is nice."

Bess snorted. "Our gardener's almost as old as we are. He can't keep up with it—it's a jungle."

Abigail emerged from the kitchen again, this time with a plate piled high with sausages.

"I hope there's something you like," Kitty said.

Chloe surveyed the full table. "I'm not sure where to begin."

"Follow my example then," said Bess. The old woman filled her plate with one of everything: a fried egg, a sausage, a piece of bacon and a waffle. She finished it off with a scoop of strawberry sauce and a generous dollop of whipped cream.

Chloe slid two waffles onto her own plate. "I'm not used

to such big breakfasts. My mom is always counting carbs or grams of fat, and my dad has to watch his cholesterol."

Abigail took her place in the fourth chair at the table. "Your great-aunts are watching their cholesterol as well," she confided. "This morning's feast is in your honor."

"*Abigail* is watching our cholesterol," Bess corrected.

Kitty reached over to pat the housekeeper's hand. "Not that we're complaining. Abby takes good care of us. But this morning's spread does make a nice change from porridge and dry toast!"

As Chloe was accepting a cup of tea from Abigail, a large portrait on the far wall of the dining room caught her eye. Bess followed her gaze across the table. "What do you think?" she asked. "Quite an imposing figure, isn't he?"

"Who is it?" Chloe asked.

"The lord of the manor himself. Our father, your great-grandfather."

Chloe studied her ancestor with interest. "He's very handsome. There's something almost—*mysterious* about him."

Kitty laughed. "He would have been very pleased to hear you say that. But I'm sure your father has told you all the old stories."

"He's mentioned him," said Chloe. "He was in a circus or something, wasn't he?"

"That's all you know about the great Dante Magnus?" Kitty asked, looking distressed.

Chloe shrugged. "Sorry, I don't remember any more than that."

"Not much more than that *to* remember," Bess said dryly. "Pass the syrup, please."

"Oh, no," said Kitty. "There's so much more! Your great-grandfather was an amazing man, one of the most talented magicians who ever lived. You can read Dante's story for yourself if you'd like, Chloe. He wrote a memoir."

"*Part* of a memoir," said Bess. "He disappeared before it was finished."

"Disappeared?" asked Chloe.

Kitty nodded slowly, her eyes wide. "A few months after that painting was commissioned, the entire carnival our father was with vanished. The police found a few things at the site where the carnival was last seen, including the painting that hangs on the first-floor landing. But that was it; there were no other clues."

"Clues? But didn't any of them *ever* show up again?"

"None of them, ever," said Kitty. "The police questioned people for months, for hundreds of miles in every direction. Our mother posted a large reward, but no one came forward. We never found out what happened. Some people say our father and his companions simply wandered north into the wilderness." The old woman's voice dropped as she leaned forward over her plate. "*I* think something more sinister happened to them."

"It's pointless to stir that all up now," said Bess, an edge to her voice. "It was almost a century ago. Dante would be long dead anyway."

"I'll find Dante's memoir for you," Kitty said to Chloe, ignoring her sister. "You can read his story for yourself."

Bess clucked her tongue in annoyance. "Don't force it on her, Kitty. I'm sure the last thing Chloe wants to do on her vacation is read a musty old memoir."

"No," Chloe protested. "I'd like to see it, really. I didn't know I had such an interesting ancestor."

Chloe helped Abigail carry the dishes into the kitchen after breakfast. When she returned to the dining room, her great-aunts were just sweeping the last crumbs off the tablecloth. "I was wondering," she began hesitantly. "I mean, my father said—would you mind if I explored the house after I got dressed?"

"Of course not. Explore to your heart's content," said Kitty.

"Thanks," said Chloe. "Also, I've been meaning to ask about the little key you sent with your invitation."

The two old women looked perplexed. "Key?" Kitty said.

"Yes, this one." Chloe unfastened the chain that hung around her neck and passed the tiny key to her great-aunt.

Kitty turned the key over in her hand. "I don't believe I've ever seen it before. Bess?"

"You say it was in the letter we sent you?" Bess asked.

"Yes. It fell out of the envelope."

Bess shook her head. "It didn't come from me. Why would I go to the trouble of mailing you a key? It wouldn't have been much use to you if you hadn't accepted our invitation. And if you accepted, why send a key when we were going to see you face-to-face?"

Abigail was still in the kitchen, wiping down the counters. "I posted the letter," the housekeeper admitted, "but it was sealed when I got it."

"The key fell out of the envelope," Chloe insisted. "Someone must have put it there."

Abigail nodded. "Well, it wouldn't be the first mystery this house has seen. Strange things happen here sometimes," she said, lowering her voice. "But then, it is a magician's house, after all."

"What do you mean, 'strange things'?"

Abigail paused, her dishrag suspended in the air. "Most of the time it's just a feeling I get—" She fell silent as the door from the dining room swung open and Bess entered the kitchen with an empty cup and saucer.

"Am I interrupting something?" Bess asked.

Abigail's plump face had gone a little pinker than usual. "Just telling Chloe what a pleasure it is to work here."

Chloe waited until her great-aunt was gone again before pressing Abigail to continue. But the housekeeper had changed her mind. "I really shouldn't be filling your head with ideas. Next thing you know you'll be seeing ghosts everywhere."

"Ghosts?"

"Now look what I've started!"

"But—"

"No," said Abigail, shaking her head. "My lips are sealed."

Feeling a little unsettled, Chloe left the kitchen to have a shower and get dressed. She was on her way to the staircase at the center of the house when she passed the doorway to the sitting room. She peered inside. It was a cozy room, filled with polished wood furniture. A chintz-covered love seat and two upholstered armchairs faced a large stone fireplace, and there was an upright piano tucked in the far corner. Chloe hesitated for only a second before crossing the room.

The lid of the piano folded back without any resistance. Chloe's heart was pounding in her chest as she looked down at the keys. She wiped her damp palms on her shorts and lifted her hands into the air. "A few scales, that's all. No one's listening." But half a minute passed and then half a minute more, and her fingers remained suspended just above the keys.

"Any luck tracing the source of your mystery key?" Bess asked from the doorway.

Chloe turned, startled. "No—not yet," she stammered.

"I didn't mean to alarm you," said her great-aunt. "I see you found our old piano. Your father said it would be like a magnet to you."

"He told you about the recital, didn't he?" Chloe said, fighting an unexpected wave of anger. "That's why you invited me here."

Bess's voice was gentle. "We *wanted* to see you, Chloe. We're not getting any younger, Kitty and I. But it is true that your parents are very concerned about you. Your father didn't tell us any of the details and we didn't pry, but we gather you had a rough experience at a performance recently."

"I haven't played in front of anyone for almost two months," Chloe said, chewing her lower lip. "I want to, but I just can't. Not even for my piano teacher. It's stupid."

"Not so stupid. Don't worry, it will happen when you're ready. You won't get any pressure from anyone in this house. As it happens, Kitty and I know a thing or two about stage fright."

"Thanks," said Chloe.

"Well, I'll leave you to it," Bess said with a nod.

When Bess was gone again, Chloe closed the piano lid and left the sitting room. She continued down the hallway to the huge oak staircase that rose up through the center of the house. On the landing between the first and second floors, she paused to study a painting that hung beside an ornate grandfather clock. "The carnival painting," Chloe murmured, remembering her great-aunts' story at breakfast. The painting showed a cluster of brightly colored tents arranged in a half-circle against a backdrop of snowcapped mountains. At the center of the tents there was a low stage with the name *Carnival des Grands Lacs* painted in elegant script at its base. There were several small figures in the picture: a tall man with a serpent around his neck, a dark man juggling half a dozen golden balls, and a tiny woman doing a handstand balanced on the raised arms of her equally short partner. Chloe looked for her great-grandfather and found him holding up a fiery ball in the shadows on the left-hand side of the stage. There was no sign of his wife or of any children.

The longer Chloe studied the painting, the more details she noticed: the horses grazing off in the distance, the snakes curled up in cages in the shadow of one of the tents, the cases of bottles on display to the left of the stage. It was all oddly compelling. Chloe ran her fingertips over the painted scene. When the grandfather clock beside her began to strike the hour, she forced her eyes away from the picture and continued up the stairs.

The long hallway at the top of the first flight of stairs was dimly lit by two small windows, one at either end. Chloe made her way to the nearest door, which opened into a bright room with pale yellow walls.

It was clear from the child-size furnishings and the many toys that filled the generous space that the room had once been a nursery. There was a table with three chairs in the far corner of the room, set with tiny china cups and saucers. A large open chest overflowing with porcelain dolls and ancient teddy bears sat in another corner of the room. A magnificent rocking horse in the center of the nursery caught Chloe's attention. She ran her fingers over the polished wooden head, the smooth leather saddle. The horse was so lifelike that Chloe half-expected to hear it give a soft whinny.

Chloe examined a few more of the antique toys, and then she turned her attention to the bookshelves that lined two walls of the room. She was immersed in an old mystery when Abigail came up to tell her that lunch was ready.

Chloe checked her watch in surprise. She'd been reading for hours. "Wow. I totally lost track of the time," she said as she rose and followed Abigail down the hall to the stairs. When she reached the landing, Chloe paused for another quick look at the painting next to the grandfather clock. "That's odd," she said, leaning in to study the picture more closely.

Abigail looked back over her shoulder. "What's that?"

"This painting. It's different. I'm almost positive that the sun is higher in the sky now, and I think the ponies have moved slightly too. And the performers are in different places." Chloe blinked and squinted at the picture again. "My eyes must be playing tricks on me."

"Or the house is," Abigail said knowingly.

Chloe looked up from the painting. "What?"

But the housekeeper just shook her head and carried on down the stairs.

Kitty was eager to hear about Chloe's explorations. Between mouthfuls of soup, Chloe described all the old books and toys she'd found in the nursery.

"We spent a good deal of our childhood playing in that room with our brother Henry, your grandfather," Kitty said.

"Found the secret passageway yet?" Bess asked.

"Secret passageway?"

"Don't give her any hints, Bess," Kitty chided. "Let her discover the house's secrets on her own. It's much more fun that way. Speaking of secrets, I found Dante's memoir." She stood up to get a book from the sideboard and placed it on the table next to Chloe's bowl.

Chloe wiped her hands carefully on her napkin before picking up the antique volume and opening it to the first page. "*The Memoirs of Dante Magnus*," she read aloud. The words were handwritten in an elegant old-fashioned script. "Thank you," said Chloe. "I'll be very careful with it, I promise."

"Take it out into the back garden," Kitty suggested. "It's quiet and shady there."

"Just don't get lost in that jungle," Bess warned. "We don't want to have to send a search party after you."

"I'll be careful," Chloe repeated, not sure how seriously to take her great-aunt.

Chapter Three

Chloe stepped outside with Dante's book tucked under her arm and immediately found herself beneath a dense floral canopy. Roses, camellias and other bushes that she couldn't identify competed for sun in the space closest to the house. Rhododendrons and huge ferns grew in the shadow of the high stone walls that enclosed the yard on two sides. The back of the garden was hidden from sight behind a thick screen of overgrown trees and shrubs.

She forced her way along a worn stone path that was really more a leafy tunnel than a trail, burrowing deeper and deeper into the garden. The tunnel curved and curved again before opening into a small mossy clearing. There was a tiny pond in the center, with a fountain in the shape of a leaping fish. Two crumbling stone benches, one in the sun and one in the shade, faced each other across the pond. Chloe stretched out along the sunny bench.

With her head propped up on one arm, Chloe thumbed through the first few pages of Dante's book. It didn't look like an easy read. The handwritten script was faded in places, and the phrases that jumped out at her seemed painfully formal and old-fashioned. But Chloe was curious enough about her great-grandfather's story to turn back to the first page and begin to read.

I was born in 1866, in a windswept corner of County Antrim, on the north coast of Ireland. I was the third of eight children, christened Daniel McBride by my Catholic parents. We were little more than peasants. We did not own the small field where our donkey grazed, nor the yard where our chickens scratched, nor even the patch of dirt where we grew cabbages and carrots and potatoes. Neither did we own our home, a two-room thatched cottage with an earthen floor and an open hearth.

When I was eleven I left school to attend my first hiring fair. We gathered in the center of town, boys and girls alike, nervously clutching our small bundles as we waited to be inspected. Wealthy farmers came from the glens and townships for miles around in search of cheap labor. Most of the men merely looked me over as they passed; a few squeezed the muscles of my arms and checked my teeth as if I were a horse or some other beast of burden. I was hired by a farmer for the standard term of six months. For six months I labored from first light until nightfall, tending the cows and pigs, carrying water, plowing and tilling the stubbled fields. I endured my master's stick when he was drunk and the rough side of his tongue when he was sober. At night I slept on a wide ledge above the cattle in the byre.

It was the practice at the end of each term to pay the mother of the child laborer the few coins that were due, but as I grew older I demanded my fee directly. I surrendered most of it to help feed my younger siblings, but I also kept a little back. By the spring of 1883, the year that I turned seventeen, I had saved enough to pay for passage to England and on to the Americas.

I secured passage from Belfast to Liverpool on a small steamship. From Liverpool it was my intention to sail directly to New York, but the quickest passage available to North America was on a ship bound for Montreal in Canada. It was fate. If I had taken any other ship, I would not have met the great American magician who introduced me to my vocation.

As Chloe grew more absorbed in her great-grandfather's story, Dante's formal language became less of a distraction. It was as if his words were dissolving into moving images, the story coming to life on the pages in front of her. She could almost smell the salt in the air and feel the deck move under her feet as Dante's ship steamed westward past the south coast of Ireland.

I was getting some air up on deck on the second day of my voyage when a tall, sandy-haired man approached from the opposite direction. After we had chatted for a few moments, my new acquaintance invited me to a show he was putting on that evening in the first-class lounge. I took a seat in an empty corner at the back of the lounge just before eight o'clock. As the oil lamps were dimmed, a man in a tuxedo stepped forward at the front of the room. "It is my great honor," he announced, "to introduce to this distinguished audience a man famous on five continents, a man who has performed in front of Queen Victoria herself—the great American magician, Mr. Harry Kellar!"

The room went black. When the lights came up again, the man who had introduced himself to me on deck stood on a raised platform at the front of the lounge. I watched, spellbound, as he performed one trick after another. He tossed a birdcage with a live dove inside it into the air, and the bird and cage both disappeared. He put tiny plants inside hollow tubes and withdrew mature rose bushes. Beneath the magician's skillful fingers, the roses disappeared, reappeared and changed color.

For his final illusion of the evening, Mr. Kellar allowed himself to be bound, gagged, tied to a chair and locked securely inside a wooden spirit cabinet. There was only space for one person inside the small cabinet, but it became clear almost immediately that the magician had been joined by some ghostly presence. Mr. Kellar's assistant knocked on the cabinet door, and in response we heard a low moan, and the curtain that hung in the cabinet's window began to ripple slightly. A ghostly arm appeared through the window, and as it was withdrawn we heard the sound of a horn, then the

clanging of a bell, then the crashing of a tambourine,
then all three instruments together.

When Kellar's assistant opened the door a few
moments later, the magician appeared before us again,
still gagged and tied to the chair, every rope in place.

I sprang to my feet instantly, overwhelmed by what
I'd just seen. "Bravo," I called out. Kellar flashed the
audience a crooked grin and bowed once he had been
freed.

The scene ended, and Chloe became aware of her sur-
roundings again. She shook her head and blinked. It had
all been so clear, as if she'd been watching a movie. She
wanted to read more, but the warm breeze playing over her
body and the soft burble of the fountain beside her made
the words on the next page blur together. Her eyelids had
grown impossibly heavy. She put the book down and let her
head drop onto her outstretched arm. A moment later she
was asleep.

She was walking through a hallway lined with mirrors.
From the neck down, her body was reflected accurately, but
a different face peered out at her from every panel. When
she stopped in front of the last mirror, she saw her own face
reflected in the glass. Then the glass rippled and a stranger's
face shimmered into view. The woman in the mirror spoke,
but no sound escaped the glass. Chloe thought she saw the
woman's lips form her name, but as hard as she tried, she
couldn't make out anything else.

Chloe woke up suddenly, the stone bench hard against
her back. For a moment she thought she heard a woman

whispering nearby, but it was only the soft hum of some bees in a honeysuckle vine. She stretched her arms and sat up.

"Come join us, dear," Kitty called from the front veranda after supper.

Chloe took a seat at the wicker table. Her great-aunts and their housekeeper sipped their tea and chatted as the sun sank in the sky, turning the canal across the street candy-floss pink. The night air was warm, but a cool breeze from the water kept the veranda from getting stuffy. Throughout the evening, passersby of all ages smiled and waved up at the women on the porch. Many of them paused to exchange a friendly word or two as well.

"Do you know *everyone* in Little Venice?" Chloe asked. "You must have introduced me to half the town already."

"Your great-aunts have been fixtures in this town for almost a century," Abigail told Chloe proudly. "Anyone who's been here more than a week knows the famous McBride sisters."

"Famous?" Chloe asked.

Bess raised one eyebrow. "Abigail's laying it on a little thick. She does that."

"I do not," the housekeeper insisted with a sniff. "Your great-aunts were famous stage actresses, Chloe. People traveled from miles around to watch them play all the starring roles at St. Mark's Theatre."

"Nothing we loved more than being on the stage," Kitty said, her eyes sparkling. "Born performers, both of us. It runs in the family, you know—there's no escaping it."

"What about my grandfather?" Chloe asked.

"Henry would have ended up on the stage too if he hadn't died so young—just after your father was conceived. He was going to be a magician, just like his father. And then there's *your* father and his saxophone."

"And Chloe McBride." Abigail beamed. "Future concert pianist!"

"Or teacher or diplomat," Bess added quickly, frowning at the housekeeper.

Chloe tried to appear indifferent, but she could feel the color rising to her face. She lifted the napkin from her lap and placed it beside her empty teacup. "I'm a little tired. I think I'll go to bed now."

"I'm so sorry," said Abigail, lifting her fingers to her mouth. "I didn't mean to upset you."

"I'm fine," Chloe insisted, forcing a smile. "I just haven't adjusted to the time difference yet."

"Of course, dear," said Kitty. "You go on in. We'll see you in the morning."

Chapter Four

It took Chloe a few seconds to remember where she was when she woke up the next morning. Sunlight was streaming through the window, and Dante's book lay open on the floor where it had fallen in the night. Chloe picked it up before going out to find her great-aunts.

"Were your dreams sweet, my dear?" Kitty asked as she poured Chloe a glass of orange juice.

"They were different," Chloe said as she accepted the glass. "I dreamt I was on a ship in the middle of a storm. And then somehow I wasn't on the ship anymore; I was trapped inside the painting on the landing."

Kitty put the pitcher of juice down. "Interesting. Your father used to dream that he was inside the painting too. He loved that picture so much that we hung it on the wall across from his bed when he stayed with us. But then he started having dreams about it every night, and we thought it would be wiser to move it back to the landing. He was becoming obsessed with it."

"Did he ever mention anything strange about it?" Chloe asked as Kitty offered her a plate of toast.

"Strange?"

Chloe looked across the table at Abigail, but the house-keeper's eyes were fixed on the toast she was buttering. "I don't know," said Chloe. "Like, did it ever seem to change slightly? As if the people in it had moved, or the sun was in a different place?"

"Abigail," Bess interjected, glaring across the dining room. "Have you been telling tales?"

"I haven't told her anything," Abigail said, her cheeks flushing. "Chloe saw what she saw."

"I don't know that I saw anything," Chloe said. "I'm sure it was just my imagination."

"There's a lot of superstitious nonsense floating around about this house," Bess told Chloe. "Don't let yourself get swept up in it. That's exactly what it is—superstitious nonsense."

After breakfast, Chloe crossed the road to the canal path and walked into the center of town. She had no particular destination in mind. She let her feet carry her down one street and up another until a tantalizing smell lured her into a shop with a bright pink and white awning. She came out a few minutes later with a generous scoop of raspberry ripple ice cream in a huge waffle cone.

Chloe retraced her steps to the stone bridge that crossed the canal. She took a seat on the edge of the wall to watch the water while she ate. She was just finishing the last few bites of her cone when a girl with sandy blond hair peeking from underneath her bike helmet braked abruptly a few feet away from Chloe. "Hi," said the girl.

"Uh, hi," said Chloe.

"You're Chloe, right?" the girl asked, resting her elbows on the handlebars of her mountain bike. "I saw you on the McBrides' porch last night. Kitty told my father you were coming to stay this summer."

"Just for a month," said Chloe, not sure what else to say.

The girl took off her sunglasses, and the corners of her wide mouth turned up in a grin. "Sorry. I'm Nyssa. You're probably wondering why Kitty was talking to my father about you, right?"

"I kind of get the impression that she's told half the town about me."

Nyssa laughed. "Probably. Anyway, Kitty was talking to my father about the vaudeville festival he's organizing at the theater at the end of July. It's an annual thing in Little Venice."

"A vaudeville festival?"

"Yeah, you know—like the old traveling shows with minstrels, comedians, magicians. Stupid animal tricks, stupid human tricks, the whole bit. It's kind of corny, but it's fun."

"My great-grandfather was a magician," said Chloe.

"I know," said Nyssa. "Your great-aunts taught me a few of his tricks to perform in the junior talent show. That's why Kitty was talking to my father about you. She wanted to know if it was too late for you to enter."

Chloe felt a familiar knot forming in her intestines. "She didn't mention it to me."

"Well, it's not too late. My father said he'd be happy to add your name to the program."

Chloe shook her head. "I can't. "

"Kitty says you're an awesome pianist," said Nyssa. "I know a junior talent show doesn't sound like much, but the prizes are pretty decent. First prize is a five-thousand-dollar scholarship."

"Wow. That's like—wow."

"I know. Some old rich guy willed a lot of money to the festival a few years ago. Pretty amazing, eh?"

"I still can't," Chloe said as her teeth found her lower lip.

"Why not?"

"I'm not really—it's just—I'm sorry," said Chloe, fumbling for a way out of the conversation. "I'm supposed to be back for lunch in ten minutes. It was nice meeting you, though."

Nyssa shrugged. "You too. I'll catch you later, I guess." She lifted her feet to the pedals of the bike and began to cycle away. "Hey! Think about it," Chloe heard her call back over her shoulder.

Chloe slipped out into the back garden after supper that evening, made herself comfortable on one of the benches and began to read the next chapter of Dante's memoir. It wasn't long before the story took hold of her again.

I was walking on the upper deck of the ship the morning after Mr. Kellar's performance when the magician suddenly came up behind me.

"Well, what did you think?" he asked.

"It was like nothing I've ever seen!" I said. "I couldn't sleep! But I was troubled by the spirit cabinet," I admitted, crossing myself quickly. "It's not right to summon things from beyond the grave!"

Kellar exploded in laughter. "Oh, my boy! I'm a magician, not a spiritualist! It's all illusion, every last bit of it. I picked up that particular trick when I was not much older than you, as a matter of fact. That it fooled you is the sincerest compliment you could ever pay me."

I felt my face flush. "Of course. I just meant—could you tell me how to become a magician?" I found myself asking in a rush.

Kellar stared at me. "How serious are you?"

"Very." My hands were trembling, but my gaze was steady.

Kellar nodded. "So, magic has claimed another victim. That's the way it was with me. One show and magic reeled me in."

"Can you teach me, then?"

"I don't think you understand what you're asking," Kellar said. "Magic isn't something you learn overnight. There's a difference between knowing how a trick is done and knowing how to do it, and learning that difference takes years."

He must have seen the disappointment in my face. He hesitated for just a moment before smiling and clapping his hand on my shoulder. "I can't give you years, but assuming the weather is favorable, we have eight days before we disembark in Montreal. I could teach you a trick or two, give you a few pointers to get you started. After that it's up to you."

True to his promise, while our ship steamed across the Atlantic, Kellar showed me how to make coins appear and disappear and how to make handkerchiefs vanish up my sleeves. I practiced day and night.

"Not bad," said Kellar. "But if you're serious about making it in this business, you'll need a new name. Something more impressive for the stage."

A new name seemed appropriate for the new life I had chosen, and so I immediately re-christened myself Dante Magnus.

On the seventh day of our voyage, Newfoundland came into view. We docked in Montreal a few days later. I begged Kellar for permission to go with him on his North American tour, but he turned me down, saying only that he already had more help than he needed. Instead he offered me a letter of introduction to a man named Dickey in a traveling show near the prairie city of Winnipeg. I took the train west and found the show set up on the banks of the Red River, just south of the city.

Circus Animagicus consisted of half a dozen tents and wagons set up in a loose half-circle. Painted wooden signboards outside each tent advertised all kinds of marvels: fire-eaters, sword swallowers, bearded women. There were only a few other people in sight as I entered the largest canvas tent. The sign outside said Dr. Inferno, Master of Mystery.

"Show's not 'til four," a skinny youth informed me.

"No admittance until three thirty."

"I'm here to see Dickey," I said, hoping I sounded more confident than I felt. "I have a letter of introduction."

The boy shrugged. "I wouldn't go looking for Dickey until at least two o'clock, if I were you. Three o'clock is safer. Oh—and if you value your Irish skin, you won't make the mistake of calling him Dickey to his face. It's Mr. Dickens, or Dr. Inferno, if you prefer."

"Thank you," I mumbled. "And where would I find Mr. Dickens after three o'clock?"

The boy gestured with a thumb over his shoulder. "In the yellow wagon, behind this tent."

I paced outside the tent, periodically looking up to check the position of the sun in the sky. When I judged that it was mid-afternoon, I approached the peeling yellow wagon behind Dr. Inferno's tent and knocked softly on the door. Half a minute passed in silence, and I knocked again with more force. This time loud thumping and banging erupted from inside the wagon.

"What is it?" a voice thundered.

"Mr. Dickens?" I said nervously. "I have a note here for you from Harry Kellar."

"From who?"

"From Mr. Kellar, the magician."

There was cursing and the sound of a latch being drawn. A grotesque head appeared in the doorway. Albert Dickens' black moustache and beard were tangled, and his swollen cheeks were webbed with tiny broken blood vessels. "Well?" he demanded, squinting into the afternoon light.

"Mr. Dickens," I stammered, taking a step down-wind of the sour alcohol on his breath. I held the envelope up.

He snatched it from my hand and tore out the letter that was inside. When he was finished reading, he looked me over and swore. "Bloody hell! The last thing I need is one of Kellar's castoffs!"

"Mr. Kellar thought you might be happy to have some assistance," I said, my voice strained.

"You got any skills?"

"I know a few coin tricks. I've still got a lot to learn, but—"

Dickens cut me off with a wave of his meaty hand. "I don't know what fantasies Kellar put into your head, but you can forget about the amateur parlor tricks he taught you. If you want to eat, you'll have to earn your keep."

My first assignment was to pick up litter from the carnival site. Half an hour before the first magic show of the day, I was called over to help collect money from the eager spectators lined up outside Dr. Inferno's tent. When I'd collected the last admission, I slipped inside the tent to watch the show myself.

Dr. Inferno stumbled out onto the stage wearing a dirty cape and a wild black wig that reached past his shoulders. His act was a disappointment from the start. Cards and coins slipped from his fingers as he was performing, and silk scarves peeked out of their *hiding places in his pockets and up his sleeves. Worst of all, with every slurred phrase he sprayed saliva over the unlucky audience members sitting in the first few rows.*

Chloe turned the page and continued reading. As bad as Dr. Inferno's magic act was, Dante was still fascinated by it. It didn't take Chloe long to figure out why. Dickens' clumsiness made it easier for Dante to see through his illusions. Dante was learning from the magician's mistakes.

I was a faithful observer at the back of Dr. Inferno's tent every afternoon and evening for three months. By the end of that period, I had succeeded in figuring out all of my employer's secrets. I improvised my own make-shift props from scavenged bits and pieces and practiced my new tricks whenever I was alone. I realized late one summer night that I had learned everything I could. There was no future for me in Circus Animagicus. Before sunrise the next morning, I was packed up and on the road.

Chloe let out an involuntary cry when someone tapped her on the shoulder, bringing her abruptly back to the present.

"Sorry. " Nyssa grinned as she dropped down on the grass a few feet away from Chloe's bench. "I didn't mean to freak you out."

"That's okay," Chloe said, trying to catch her breath.

"Must be good, what you're reading. You were really zoned out. I said your name twice, but you didn't hear me."

Chloe closed the book. "It's my great-grandfather's memoir. It's weird," she said, shaking her head. "I kind of go into a trance when I start reading it. It's like watching a movie or something."

"Dante Magnus? That's his memoir?"

Chloe nodded. "Right—I forgot you know who he is."

"When my father told your great-aunts I was interested in magic, they invited me over and taught me a few things that their mother had passed on to them. Just a few basic tricks that she learned before Dante disappeared, but it got me started."

"Dante had to start from scratch too," said Chloe, "and he became famous. Or so I'm told. I haven't got that far in the story yet."

"He's in *The Magician's Encyclopedia*," Nyssa said. "But I didn't know he'd published a memoir."

"He didn't publish it. This is his handwritten manuscript."

"Cool. I won't keep you from it," Nyssa said as she pushed herself up from the grass. She pulled a folded piece of paper out of the back pocket of her shorts and held it out to Chloe. "I just came by to give you this."

It was an entry form for the Little Venice Junior Talent Show. Chloe folded it up again and slipped it between the pages of Dante's book. "Thank you," she said, trying to keep her voice light. "But why are you encouraging the competition?"

"We'd be entered in different categories," said Nyssa. "Anyway, I'm just doing the show for fun. Not like you— you've got prize potential."

"No, I don't," said Chloe, shaking her head quickly.

"Don't be modest. You've been playing the piano since you were, like, three, according to Kitty. I know the judges. Just play a few period pieces, some ragtime or something, and they'll love you."

"Look, I know you mean well, but you've got the wrong girl," said Chloe. "You want to know the truth? I haven't played in front of anybody in two months. I mean *anybody*. I couldn't even play a scale in front of my parents right now if you paid me."

"Why not?" Nyssa asked.

Chloe shut her eyes. Her heart had begun to race as she saw herself back on stage again.

"Sorry. I didn't mean to be pushy. If you don't want to talk about it, I understand," Nyssa said after a moment.

"It was just a recital," Chloe said angrily, her eyes still closed. "That's all it was. I've been performing at recitals since I was five. It shouldn't have mattered that it was being recorded for a radio broadcast. It was important, but so what? I was *ready* for it."

Nyssa remained silent.

"It was a nightmare," Chloe said, her voice faltering. "My brain froze; my fingers were like wood. Chopin's Nocturne in F-sharp Major is challenging, but I *knew* it. I should have been able to play it blindfolded, but my mind just went blank. The notes were just black squiggles on the page."

"What did you do?" Nyssa asked quietly.

"What did I do? I just sat there sweating and shaking like a complete idiot. For all I know I was drooling! Then I ran from the stage and threw up. It was the most humiliating experience of my life."

"Lots of people get stage fright, you know," Nyssa said. "Even the professionals. You should hear the stories my dad tells. You'd never guess what some actors go through behind the scenes. Stage fright is just a fact of life for lots of performers."

"You don't understand," Chloe insisted. "Stage fright cannot be 'just a fact of life' if it prevents me from performing at all. My parents sent me to see a therapist, but it's not helping. I'm supposed to work at 'visualizing' a successful performance. But every time I imagine playing in front of someone, my heart starts to race, and my palms get sweaty, and I feel sick to my stomach. This isn't just a case of the jitters, okay? And the worst thing is, all I've *ever* wanted to be is a concert pianist. Since I was, like, five years old. I can't even *imagine* doing anything else."

Nyssa was silent for a few seconds. "Come on," she said suddenly, grabbing Chloe's arm. "There's a piano in your great-aunts' house, right?"

"Yes, but I *can't*—"

"One note," said Nyssa. "Just one, that's all. Any note you want."

"No—"

"Come on. It's all right."

Chloe yanked her arm free. "I said I'm not ready yet!"

"*Sorry*," said Nyssa, holding up her hands in surrender. "Just trying to help."

"I know. I'm sorry," said Chloe. She took a deep breath. "It's just, when I feel pressured, it makes it worse. I know I sound like a mental case, but I have to get through this my own way."

Nyssa shrugged. "Well, when you're ready, I'm there. I'd be impressed no matter what you played. Really. I can't even play *Chopsticks*."

Chloe nodded and attempted a smile. "Thanks, I think."

Chapter Five

"I dreamt that someone was playing our old piano in the wee hours of the morning," Kitty said at breakfast the next day.

Chloe felt her face flush. She remained silent, concentrating on the pattern the maple syrup made as she drizzled it over her pancakes. Out of the corner of her eye, she saw Bess give her twin a pointed look.

"Wasn't half bad for a dream," Kitty said, ignoring her sister.

After breakfast, Chloe returned to the second floor to continue exploring the house. On her way upstairs, she paused to check the painting on the first landing. "It's changed—it's not my imagination!" she said, backing away in surprise. The cluster of tents was the same, but the landscape behind them was definitely different. The snow on the mountain

peaks had disappeared, and the peaks themselves had soft-
ened into gently rolling hills.

"It's a magician's house," Chloe reminded herself. It had
to be an illusion; maybe it was just the way the light hit the
canvas at different times of the day. She took a few breaths
to steady herself and continued up the stairs.

Chloe returned to the nursery, determined to find the
secret passageway Bess had mentioned, as well as the lock
that would open with her tiny key. She tackled the room
systematically this time, mentally dividing it into squares in
a grid. Starting under the south window and working her
way slowly counterclockwise, Chloe examined every toy
and every piece of furniture in her path, including a small
music box that played a different tinny tune every time she
opened it. There was no sign of a locked journal or chest
that might welcome her key. As she made her way around
the room, she carefully checked for loose floorboards and
tested shelves and wall panels for signs of a hidden latch or
door.

The better part of an hour had passed before she turned
her attention to the bookcases that lined two walls of the
nursery. Chloe pushed and pulled each section of the bookcases, but they remained fixed in place. As a last resort, she
began removing books from the shelves. She emptied one
shelf at a time, and then she replaced the books in the order
that she'd found them before moving on to the next shelf.
She glanced at the cover of each book as she removed it and
quickly thumbed through its pages, just in case one of the
volumes had been hollowed out and converted into a tiny
treasure box or safe.

Chloe removed volumes A through P of a set of antique encyclopedias, but when she reached for volume Q, she found that it was stuck. Volumes R through Z slipped out without any difficulty, but volume Q remained fixed on the shelf, upright, all alone. Chloe couldn't see anything holding the leather-bound book in place, so she tugged a little harder. This time the top of the book tilted backward slightly, as if on a hinge. There was a distinct *click*, and the section of the bookcase directly in front of Chloe moved. She pushed the shelves gently and they began to turn, revealing a widening crack of gray light from the next room.

When a wide-enough opening had been created, Chloe squeezed through and found herself in a room that was about half the size of the nursery. Dusty sports pennants hung on the wall above a single bed, and black-and-white photographs of uniformed schoolboys sat on a wooden desk. Chloe picked up the nearest photograph. There were no familiar faces among the young men who stared back at her, their arms folded across their chests.

"There you are," a voice called from the far side of the room.

Chloe jumped, and then she relaxed again when she saw that it was only Abigail, peering in from the other side of the opening.

"I see you found the secret passageway into Henry's room."

"This was my grandfather's bedroom?"

"Yes. Not much has changed since he left," the house-keeper said. "Going on seven decades now." She made a clucking sound with her tongue. "What this house needs is a good clearing out. Get rid of all the cobwebs and ghosts in one fell swoop."

"Ghosts?" Chloe asked, her eyebrows rising hopefully.

Abigail lifted her hand to her mouth, her eyes wide. "Sorry—just an expression. I came to tell you that two hungry women and a plate of grilled cheese sandwiches are waiting downstairs for you."

Chloe was helping Abigail with the dishes after dinner that evening when Nyssa appeared at the back door.

"Want to ride down to the lake with me?" Nyssa asked.

"I don't have a bike," said Chloe.

"No problem. I can double you."

"Go on," said Abigail. "Just a few pots left anyway."

Chloe dried her hands and went to tell her aunts where she was going. She followed Nyssa outside and around to the front of the house where Nyssa's bike was leaning against the gate.

"Hold on tight," Nyssa said as Chloe climbed onto the bike behind her. "It's all downhill from here."

"I've got something I want to show you," Nyssa told Chloe when they reached the beach a few minutes later.

"What?" Chloe asked as she sat down on a log.

Nyssa reached into her backpack and brought out a deck of cards, a small black box, a plastic container and a wand. "I'm still working on this," she warned as she opened the plastic container to reveal three eggs, "so don't expect too much. It's one of the tricks your great-aunts taught me."

"Really? One of Dante's tricks?"

"It was one of the tricks that Dante performed, but he didn't invent it. Lots of magicians do this one. Houdini even did it."

"Cool," said Chloe, leaning forward.

Nyssa cleared her throat. "Okay, here we go." She shuffled the pack of cards, and then she fanned them out, facedown, in front of Chloe. "Take one. Don't show it to me; just tear it up."

"Like this?" Chloe asked as she tore a Jack of Spades into half a dozen pieces.

"That's right. Now put the pieces in the black box."

When the torn pieces were inside the box, Nyssa closed the lid. "Wait, I forgot." She opened the box again and put her hand inside. She withdrew a single torn corner and handed it to Chloe. "Take this and hold on to it. At my command, I'm going to make the rest of the card appear inside the egg of your choice."

"Really?" Chloe said skeptically. "And how are you going to do that?"

"C'mon," said Nyssa. "Just choose an egg."

Chloe pointed at one of the three eggs.

"Good. Now remove the other two eggs."

As Chloe obeyed, Nyssa held up her wand and waved it three times over the sealed black box. She whispered an incantation and jabbed the air above the egg that Chloe had selected. "Now watch carefully," Nyssa commanded her friend.

Chloe watched as Nyssa forced the tip of her wand through the egg's shell, breaking it open. A rolled-up card emerged from the gooey interior of the egg. "Can I pick it up?" Chloe asked.

Nyssa nodded, and Chloe pulled the card out, wiping it off against the edge of the container. "It's my card," she said in amazement. "But it's in one piece! It's just missing the corner I'm holding in my hand!"

"Do they match—the piece that's missing and the piece you tore off?" Nyssa asked.

"You know they do," said Chloe. "How did you *do* that? That was amazing!"

Nyssa gave a shallow bow. "Thank you. A magician doesn't usually tell her secrets, but I'll make an exception for you. After all, you *are* the great-granddaughter of Dante Magnus. First, the card you tore up is still in the bottom of the box. It's a trick box with a secret compartment. I only pretended to take out the torn corner that I gave to you. That piece really came from a second card."

"Okay," said Chloe, "but how did *that* card get inside the egg?"

"The second card was rolled up inside my hollow wand. At the same time I was breaking the egg, I was forcing the card out with a rod hidden inside the wand. It all happened at once, but you couldn't see it because of the bits of shell and the broken egg yolk in the way."

"I get it," Chloe said, nodding slowly. "Except how did you know which card I was going to choose?"

"That was the easiest part." Nyssa grinned and held up the pack of cards. She fanned them out, face up this time.

Chloe groaned. "They're *all* the Jack of Spades."

"There, I've let you in on one of my best tricks. Now

you owe me," Nyssa said as she began gathering up her props.

Chloe handed her friend the two unbroken eggs. "Owe you what?" she asked suspiciously.

"Don't panic. I don't want your money. I just want to know what it's really like, staying in Dante Magnus's house. People say it's haunted, you know."

Chloe felt goose bumps rise on her arms. "Haunted? Like how?"

Nyssa shrugged her shoulders. "Mostly it's just what kids say. You know. Any house that big and that old has got to be good for a few ghost stories."

"Do they say anything about Dante's disappearance?"

Nyssa zipped her backpack and sat down again. "According to most of the stories, Dante didn't really disappear. They say he's either hiding or trapped somewhere in the house."

"He'd be long dead by now," said Chloe. "He was in his early fifties when he vanished, and that was, like, almost a century ago."

"Well, his bones then."

It was a warm evening, but Chloe shivered anyway.

"Sorry," said Nyssa. "Didn't mean to freak you out. It's just a story kids tell when they're bored."

"I don't know." Chloe rubbed her hands over her arms. "There are some weird things going on in that house."

"Like what?"

"Like this, for starters." Chloe held up the tiny key hanging from the chain around her neck. "It came with the invitation my great-aunts sent me. Thing is, no one seems to know what it's for or how it got into the envelope."

"Okay, that's a little creepy, but *someone* must have put it there. Is there anything else?"

"What about a picture that changes every time I go past?" said Chloe.

Nyssa listened to Chloe's description of the painting of the carnival on the first-floor landing. "Maybe the painting just looks different as the light changes," she suggested when Chloe was finished. "Kind of like an early hologram."

"Is that even possible?"

"I don't know," Nyssa said. "But there has to be some kind of rational explanation. Like the obvious one, maybe, that someone is switching them on you as a practical joke."

Chloe shook her head. "But who would do that? And why?"

Nyssa shrugged. "No idea. You're the one staying there."

"Okay, let's say there's an explanation for the painting and the key. But what about the dreams I've been having?" Chloe demanded. "Ever since I arrived in Little Venice, I keep dreaming that someone's trying to send me some kind of message. And then there's Dante's book. It's like a *waking* dream; I almost get hypnotized every time I start reading it."

"You're obviously a very suggestible person with a fantastic imagination," said Nyssa.

Chloe didn't even try to keep the irritation out of her voice. "Easy for *you* to say. You're not the one having weird dreams day and night." She stood up. "The sun's almost down. I'd better get back."

"Sorry," said Nyssa. "If I'd known your aunts' house was such a touchy subject, I never would have brought it up."

Chloe shook her head. "I'm sorry," she said as she fingered the key hanging at her throat. "No matter how crazy it sounds to you, there *is* something going on in that house. There's a reason I'm here this summer; I can feel it. If I could just find the lock that goes with this key, I know it would all start to make sense."

Chapter Six

Chloe was still feeling a little unsettled when she took Dante's book to bed with her that night. Her conversation with Nyssa had made her more determined than ever to finish Dante's story, even if reading the memoir was a slightly disconcerting experience. She opened the book to the next chapter and immediately entered the story.

When I left Circus Animagicus, it was my intention to find a magician who would be willing to take me under his wing until I had enough experience and enough money to launch my own act. I expected it would take a year or two at most to accomplish what I wanted. But somehow more than a decade flew past in a blur of canvas tents, crowded railcars and musty theaters. I made my way from one touring show to another, always working in the shadows of other performers. The money I earned assisting magicians or performing ten-minute crowd teasers on the vaudeville circuits was not nearly enough to buy the elaborate props, costumes and promotional materials I needed to introduce myself properly on the world stage. I became increasingly frustrated, but I did not give up. I whispered the same words over and over again before I fell asleep each night: "I will be the world's greatest magician. I will be the world's greatest magician."

I was performing with a traveling show in Vancouver in the summer of 1897 when I heard the news of the Klondike gold strike. I was ecstatic. Here at last was my chance to get the money I needed to produce my own show! Three other men agreed to travel with me to Dawson City in the Yukon: Thomas Rankin, a juggler and fire-breather; Li Yung, a knife thrower; and Antoine Langlade, a snake charmer.

In spite of our impatience to be underway, it took us the better part of a month to complete the necessary arrangements for our expedition. In mid-August we finally made our way down to the wharf with our provisions—two-thousand-pound "outfits" that consisted of enough food, clothing and essential gear to last each of us an entire year.

It was a difficult journey from the beginning. Our steamship was designed to carry fifty or sixty passengers, but there were more than four hundred people crammed on board for the voyage north. When we were still many hundreds of miles from our final destination, the ship anchored at the end of a long inlet on the Alaskan coast, at the makeshift settlement of Dyea.

Twice a day for the next three months, the four of us and countless others trekked back and forth through the rain and mud with fifty-pound loads on our backs. When we had succeeded in carrying all of our provisions from Dyea to the base camp at the foot of the Chilkoot Pass, it was time to tackle the dreaded pass itself. Earlier trekkers had carved an icy staircase of over a thousand steps into the steep mountain. After resting for a few days, my companions and I made our first ascent up what was called the "Golden Staircase." It took us almost six hours to reach the top. Over the next month and a half, we each repeated this climb forty times.

Six months after we'd left Vancouver, our group finally stood together on the far side of the Chilkoot Pass. We looked like walking corpses. Our cheeks were hollow, our beards were ragged and our clothing was shredded and filthy. But if we were exhausted, we were also thrilled to have survived.

We slid down to Lake Bennett on homemade sleds, laughing all the way. Our journey was temporarily interrupted when we were forced to set up camp on the frozen lakeshore for the next four months. While we waited for the spring thaw, we built a boat that would carry us down the Yukon River the rest of the way to Dawson. There were a few close calls during the last watery phase of our journey, but on the ninth of June, *ten months after setting out from Vancouver, the boat we'd built carried us around the last rocky outcropping. We let out a cheer. There, stretched out for miles along the bank, was the fabled Dawson City.*

In truth, my companions and I had expected something more than the mud-clogged roads, dirty shacks and weathered tents that greeted us, but we got over our disappointment quickly. We weren't there for the city; we were there to find gold. We lost no time unpacking our shovels and racing for the creeks to stake our claims.

"You're too late, cheechakos," someone jeered as we passed. It was the name, we soon learned, that locals called newcomers. "It's all gone. There's nothing left!" the voice shouted after us.

We spent two entire days trying to disprove the old sourdough's words. Eventually the truth sank in. The countryside had been staked for miles in every direction. There was nothing left to claim.

But I wasn't ready to give up. "There's more than one way to collect gold," I assured the others as we conferred by our tent. "Let the claim holders break their backs digging it out of the ground. We'll get our share another way."

"What do you have in mind?" Thomas asked suspiciously. "You aren't planning on stealing it, are you? Making it 'disappear'?"

I smiled. "A little sleight of hand, perhaps, but no stealing. Look around and what do you see? Men, thousands of them. Tired prospectors with too much money, and discouraged cheechakos like us with not enough.

What we all have in common is a need for some diversion, some entertainment. There are fortunes to be made in the Klondike, my friends. And not all of them will be dug out with shovels!"

We appointed Antoine our stage manager and assistant. He and Thomas sold our mining equipment and used the proceeds to purchase props and more presentable clothing. After we'd shaved our beards and trimmed each other's hair, we set out together to find a suitable venue for our first performance in Dawson City. We distributed handbills to every person we met, and two nights later we performed in front of a packed audience in the town hall.

The crowd was wildly appreciative from the start. Thomas had barely got his first dish in the air when a tipsy Klondiker near the front started clapping. It was contagious. By the climax of Thomas's act, as he juggled half a dozen bottles of champagne, the entire audience was on its feet. The cheering intensified when Li and Antoine appeared on the platform together and took their places ten paces apart. It was only as Li held up his first knife that the audience fell temporarily silent. When the last of a dozen knives was embedded in the wall behind Antoine, they began hooting and hollering again until the entire hall was shaking.

I jumped on stage just as Li and Antoine were making their exit. "Good evening, ladies and gentlemen," I cried. By now the crowd had worked itself into a frenzy, fueled by liquor and exhaustion. It was like yelling into a thunderstorm.

Thomas joined me on stage. "We've got to get out of here," he shouted. "This place is about to explode!"

"These people paid for three acts, and I haven't performed the third act yet," I yelled back.

"They're not even aware you're up here anymore. Look at them! They're about to riot!"

"I'd better get their attention quickly, then," I said. I raised my hands, and flames appeared at my fingertips, accompanied by a deafening clap of thunder. The hall immediately fell silent as every eye turned to the stage to watch me manipulate the flames into one large ball of fire that seemed to hover just above my outstretched palms. My hands moved, and the flaming orb moved with them. I traced slow circles in the air, and then I clapped my hands abruptly to make the orb disappear.

Next I withdrew a small case from my cloak and beckoned Thomas to join me again. I saw a mixture of surprise and fear in Thomas's eyes as I opened the case and took out a small gun.

Thomas shook his head. "No, Dante. You never said anything about performing the 'bullet catch' tonight. It's too dangerous!"

I ignored him. I was already holding the gun in the air and calling for a volunteer from the spellbound audience. A dozen men raised their hands. I pointed to a bearded man who looked slightly less ragged than the other trekkers and prospectors around him. The crowd parted in front of him, and he climbed onto the stage.

"Sir," I pronounced in a voice that carried to the very back of the hall, "I have in my hands a pistol. It is a real firearm, loaded with a single live bullet. For the benefit of the audience, would you please inspect this pistol and the ammunition inside it." When the volunteer was finished his inspection, I took the gun back and unloaded the bullet from its chamber. "I will now ask you to mark this bullet for the purposes of identification," I said. I waited while the man withdrew a small knife from his pocket and scratched something on the bullet. As the man watched, I returned the bullet to its chamber. "Thank you," I said, bowing slightly. "If you would now hand this pistol to my assistant and stand off to the side, I will prepare to perform the most amazing feat any magician has ever undertaken.

"Ladies and gentlemen," I said when Thomas had received the gun, "pay close attention. My partner will fire the pistol, and I will catch the bullet in my teeth. The danger you perceive is real. My life depends on my partner's steady hand and my own skill. Any error, no matter how slight, could prove fatal."

With trembling hands, Thomas raised the pistol. I crossed myself and nodded to show that I was ready. I saw Thomas close his eyes, and his lips moved for a moment. Then he opened his eyes again and took aim. I crumpled to the floor the instant the shot rang out. For the benefit of the audience, I waited a few seconds before staggering to my feet again. I opened my lips to reveal the bullet held between my teeth. Then I spat the bullet onto a plate and called my volunteer back on stage to verify that it was the same one.

"That's it," the bearded man said in amazement.

"*That's the bullet I marked.*" *That was all the audience needed to hear. The hall erupted in cheering and loud applause.*

After that performance, my companions and I had no trouble drawing eager crowds. We rotated our way through one venue after another: saloons, beer parlors, dance halls and theaters. But as the gold rush peaked and passed, our audiences began to dwindle. In the spring of 1900, we made the decision to return to civilization with the wealth we had accumulated. We boarded a steamship and sailed south to Vancouver, eagerly discussing plans for the next chapter of our lives.

Chloe found herself abruptly back in the present, staring at the blank space that followed the end of the last passage. She thumbed through the remaining pages of Dante's book. They were all blank. Dante had written nothing more.

Chapter Seven

"But there has to be more," Chloe insisted when she joined her great-aunts at breakfast the next morning. "Dante's story can't end in Vancouver. What about you? What about this house?"

"Dante's story doesn't end there," Kitty agreed as she spooned sugar into her tea. "Unfortunately, what you read is all he managed to record before he disappeared. I'm sure he meant to finish it."

"What happened after he left the Klondike? Did he start his own show? When did he meet your mother?"

Kitty smiled. "Even from this distance he's charmed you, hasn't he? That's one thing Dante was especially good at, charming people."

Bess dabbed at her lips with a napkin and abruptly stood up from the table. "There was nothing charming about our father's behavior. He abandoned his wife and children without a word. It's not a fairy tale, Kitty. Why you're dredging up the past at all is beyond me."

"I'm sorry," Chloe said, horrified. But Bess was already halfway through the door.

"Oh, don't mind her," Kitty said, reaching over to pat Chloe's hand. "Bess has never really forgiven our father. She bristles every time his name comes up, even all these years later. But don't worry—she may be a little annoyed with me, but she's not angry at you."

"I didn't mean to pry," said Chloe. "I'm sorry."

"Nonsense," said Kitty. "You have every right to know your family history. That's why I gave you Dante's memoir in the first place." The old woman paused to take a sip of her tea. "As to what happened after Dante returned to Vancouver, I can only tell you what our father told our mother and what she passed on to us. Dante asked his companions to join him in forming a new traveling show. The company grew as they traveled east by rail over the prairies. By the time they reached the Great Lakes, Dante had founded the *Carnival des Grands Lacs.*"

Chloe shifted in her seat. "It must have been successful, if he built this house."

"It was reasonably successful, financially speaking," said Kitty. "Dante was very good with money. He paid his performers fairly and invested the rest in timber and sawmills and mines. He did very well. He could have retired quite comfortably after just a few years on the road."

"But Dante didn't retire, did he?" Chloe asked.

"No. It wasn't money Dante was after; it was fame. He was still determined to become the world's greatest magician."

"When did he meet your mother?" Chloe asked.

"Well, now that's a story," Kitty said with a smile. "In 1909, our mother, Magdala, was working as a servant for a wealthy family in Toronto. It wasn't Magdala's idea to visit the carnival when it came to town—one of the other servants she worked with talked her into it."

"And Magdala saw Dante perform and fell in love with him," Chloe concluded.

Kitty laughed. "It wasn't just our mother who fell in love with Dante—almost every woman who saw him fell under his spell. Dante was already in his early forties by this time, but he was still quite a presence. Remember, my dear, this was before the age of movie stars. It was a rare thing to see such a handsome man, such a talented performer." Kitty's eyes had gone soft as she stared at a point somewhere past Chloe's shoulder. "Dante's act was pure enchantment. He threw scarves into the air and they became doves. He walked through a full-length mirror and disappeared. When Magdala was in the audience on that spring day in 1909, he invited her to sit in an ornate chair on stage and made the chair levitate and spin. As the chair descended, rose petals fell from the air all over our mother. She was spellbound, of course."

Bess appeared suddenly in the doorway, her hands on her hips. "Spellbound, enchantment! Really, Kitty, if you're going to tell our parents' story, the least you can do is leave out all the romantic nonsense."

"Were you listening at the door?" said Kitty.

"I was not," said Bess. "Since Abigail is out this morning, I was tidying up the kitchen. You project your voice as if you were still on the stage, Kitty. I couldn't block it out if I wanted to."

"Well, then," Kitty said, "if you don't like the way I'm telling the story, why don't *you* tell it?"

Bess was already taking her seat again. "I will." She sniffed. "It's the only way Chloe is going to hear anything like the truth. Now where had you left off?"

"Magdala had just seen Dante's act for the first time," said Chloe.

"Ah, yes," said Bess. "Despite what Kitty said about Magdala falling under Dante's spell, our mother was quite a sensible young woman. She wasn't one of those swooners or heart-clutchers. Maybe that's what our father saw in her: someone practical to balance his own rash and reckless nature."

"The fact that she was so young and pretty probably didn't hurt, either," Kitty interrupted.

"At any rate, Magdala didn't pursue Dante," said Bess. "It was very much the other way around."

Kitty nodded, her eyes bright. "Dante brought her flowers, took her out for evening meals, arranged mid-day picnics in the park. He was very persistent. He called on Magdala every day for two weeks, and then he proposed. She said yes, of course."

Bess snorted. "He was persistent, all right. He wore her down—what else could she say?"

"Oh, Bess," said Kitty, "you know very well that Magdala was happy at the beginning. They both were. Their love was real."

"And when were you born?" Chloe asked.

"In 1912," said Bess. "No one knew Magdala was pregnant with twins. Kitty shocked everyone when she emerged right after me."

"And I've been shocking people ever since," Kitty told Chloe with a wink.

"This house had just been completed a few months before," Bess continued. "It was Dante's idea to build a house this grand, certainly not Magdala's. We didn't spend much time in it as a family. Within a year, Dante was back on the road again."

"After just a few months, Magdala gathered up our things and we caught up with the carnival," said Kitty. "She didn't like being separated from Dante."

"Was it hard being on the road when you were so young?" Chloe asked.

Kitty shook her head. "Oh, no, my dear. It was quite wonderful. They spoiled us, all the other performers. It was like traveling with a large extended family."

"We were happy," Bess admitted. "We had everything we needed, and more. If only Dante had been satisfied, our childhood would have been quite idyllic."

"But why wasn't he happy?" asked Chloe. "What more did he want?"

Bess clucked her tongue angrily. "Only the world, my dear. By unhappy coincidence, Dante's dissatisfaction began the year we were born. That was the year Dante traveled down to New York to see Harry Kellar. By this time, Kellar was widely recognized as 'America's Greatest Magician.' Dante had heard a rumor that Kellar was about to retire and was looking for a successor, so he arranged a meeting with him in New York. When Dante came home again, he was full of lofty plans. He was convinced that Kellar was going to write and invite him to be his protégé."

"But the letter never came," said Kitty. "A few months later, when he learned that Kellar had chosen another magician to be his successor, Dante was absolutely heartbroken. At least that's what our mother told us."

Bess snorted. "Dante indulged his grief like a spoiled child. He retreated to the library and didn't come out for two whole weeks."

"But he did finally come out," said Kitty.

"Yes, he did," said Bess. "But he came out a man obsessed. Dante was more determined than ever to become the world's greatest magician. And we all paid the price for that."

Chloe waited for Bess to explain, but both women had fallen silent, staring into their teacups. "Did Dante's obsession have anything to do with the carnival's disappearance?" Chloe asked at last.

"Of course it did," said Bess.

"Now, we don't know that for sure," said Kitty. "What about Monsieur Lucien and his wishing box?"

"Monsieur Lucien!" Bess grimaced. "You don't still believe that fairy tale!"

Kitty sat up as tall as her tiny frame would allow. "Monsieur Lucien existed, Bess. And you can't say he wasn't an influence on our father."

"Oh, he was an influence on Dante, all right," Bess agreed. "But all that nonsense about a magical wishing box—surely even you can see what *that* was. Our mother told us that story to gloss over the ugliness of what really happened. Our father abandoned us, Kitty!"

Kitty took a deep breath before turning to Chloe. "So much time has passed," she said quietly. "It's hard to see things clearly now. Bess may be right; I don't know anymore. I suppose the best we can do is tell you what our mother told us and what we remember ourselves. You'll have to draw your own conclusions."

Chloe looked from Kitty to Bess and nodded.

"We were just five years old when Monsieur Lucien wormed his way into our lives," said Kitty. The old woman closed her eyes. "It's been almost a century, but I can still see him clearly in my mind. He was tall and slender and very formally dressed. I remember he carried an ornate gold and ebony cane. He was dark-haired, and he spoke with an accent. There was something very troubling about his eyes. They were like bottomless black pits. The first time he looked at me, I was afraid I was going to fall into them. After that I hid behind my mother whenever he was near. Bess was braver," Kitty said, opening her eyes again.

"I didn't like him," said Bess, "but I wasn't afraid of him. I was there when he presented Dante with the small wooden chest made of rosewood that he called a wishing box. It was just another magician's illusion, of course—it had to be—but Monsieur Lucien claimed that it was something more and offered to sell it to Dante after demonstrating its powers."

"Powers?" Chloe asked, leaning forward in her chair.

"Dante wrote something down on a piece of paper and locked it in the rosewood box. When he unlocked the box, he found a velvet bag full of gold coins. He believed that his wish had been granted."

"So it worked," said Chloe.

Bess gave a mirthless laugh. "That's what Dante believed. Our father was taken in by a con man, Chloe, a common crook."

"Bess wasn't the only one who didn't like Monsieur Lucien," said Kitty. "Our mother was uncomfortable around him from the very beginning. And then when she read in a newspaper that a man in a nearby city had been robbed of a collection of antique coins that matched the description of the coins in the velvet bag—well, she was *really* upset then. She confronted Dante and demanded that he send our foreign guest packing, but Dante refused. Monsieur Lucien was very persuasive. He'd already convinced Dante to make another wish, a wish for a new illusion so spectacular that it would make all his previous illusions look like amateur parlor tricks."

"I was there when that wish came true too," Bess said darkly. "At the end of his afternoon performance, Dante surrounded himself with a wall of fire. I watched from the back of the tent as my father's body seemed to catch fire and burn. I was terrified. Dante's flesh melted into a steaming, bubbling pool. I screamed, and my mother found me and pulled me into her skirts. A moment later, she forced me to turn around and look toward the stage. The smoke had cleared and Dante was visible again, whole and unhurt, like a phoenix risen from the ashes." Bess let out a long breath. "It was the most terrifying thing I'd ever seen. I had nightmares about it for years."

Kitty nodded sympathetically. "I wasn't there for that illusion, but I was there the next day when one of the performers caught fire for real. Thomas the juggler had been practicing his routine with flaming clubs. One of the clubs got away and landed at a female performer's feet. Her long dress went up like a torch. It happened so fast, I just stood there in shock. Someone knocked her to the ground and rolled with her to extinguish the flames, but she'd been badly burned. They had to rush her off to the hospital."

"I'm not sure why," said Bess, "but in our mother's mind there was some kind of connection between the illusion Dante had wished for and the accident. Maybe it was just because she was so shaken up. Those were difficult times for the whole country. World War I was raging in Europe, and Canada was shipping men overseas by the thousands. Dante was too old for military service, but many of the younger carnival performers had signed up. It was hard on everyone, waiting for news from the front to hear who was still alive and who was dead."

"Our mother must have reached the breaking point when she found out she was pregnant again," said Kitty. "She couldn't do anything about the war, but she did try to get rid of Monsieur Lucien. She gave our father an ultimatum: Tell Lucien to take his rosewood box and go, or she'd pack us up and we'd leave the carnival."

Bess shook her head. "And the foolish man chose to let Monsieur Lucien stay."

"Maybe he thought your mother was bluffing," Chloe offered.

"Dante wasn't choosing Monsieur Lucien over us forever, Bess," Kitty said to her sister. "It was supposed to be temporary. We were going to be reunited at the end of the season."

"But it wasn't temporary, was it?" Bess said angrily. "The carnival disappeared. We never saw our father again!"

"Something must have happened," Kitty insisted. "He would have returned if it were possible. He didn't abandon us of his own free will. I refuse to believe that, no matter what you say, Bess!"

The two old women glared at each other across the table.

"What *did* happen?" Chloe asked nervously.

Bess shook her head at last and turned to Chloe. "Dante was supposed to be home on the ninth of December. When he still wasn't home on the eleventh, our mother went to the police. They waited a few days to take action, but when there was still no news of Dante, they visited the site of the carnival's last engagement. They found a few posters and the painting that hangs on the landing, but nothing else."

"That's not true," Kitty interrupted. "They also found Monsieur Lucien's rosewood box."

Chloe's hand rose instantly to the key that hung at her throat. "Then you still have the wishing box?"

"Oh, no," Kitty said, shaking her head. "Our mother destroyed it as soon as the police released it to her. I'm sure that's why Bess forgot about it."

Bess had pushed herself up from the table again. "I would forget the whole darn thing if you'd only let me, Kitty. I still don't see the point in raking up the past."

Kitty winked at Chloe the moment Bess was gone. "Don't let her fool you. I knew she'd be back when I started telling you Dante and Magdala's story. Bess wants you to know your family history every bit as much as I do."

Chapter Eight

Nyssa showed up at the door after lunch. "What are you up to this afternoon?" she asked Chloe. "Want to walk into town?"

Chloe's fingers were wrapped around the key at her neck. "Actually, I was just on my way upstairs."

"To look for your mystery lock? Even better," said Nyssa. "I've never been past the main floor. I've always wanted to see the rest of the house."

When Chloe hesitated, Nyssa put up her hands. "I'll be cool. I won't say anything more about haunted houses, I promise."

"All right," said Chloe. She stepped back to let her friend enter. "We can cover more ground with two pairs of eyes anyway." On their way up the stairs, Chloe pointed out the painting of the carnival on the first landing.

"This is it?" said Nyssa, leaning forward to get a better look. "This is the picture that keeps changing?"

Chloe nodded. "And now look, there's a lake in the background. I swear that's the first time I've seen the lake. No matter what you say about holograms or practical jokes, this picture still creeps me out!"

Nyssa studied the painting a second longer. "All right then, let's see if this lake is still here when we come back downstairs."

A minute later they were on the third floor, entering a storage room lined with cupboards and shelves and wardrobes. Garment racks filled most of the center of the room.

"Cool," Nyssa said as Chloe unzipped the nearest garment bag and removed a long gown of gauzy white fabric. Nyssa reached for the handle of the mahogany wardrobe beside her. She was almost buried in the avalanche of garments that spilled out when she opened the door. "Wow. Did all these costumes come from Dante's carnival?" she asked.

"All that stuff disappeared with Dante, I think," said Chloe. "Kitty told me that her mother was a seamstress and costume maker for St. Mark's."

"Your great-grandmother *made* these?" said Nyssa, holding up a mermaid's tail covered with glittering scales. "That is so cool."

Chloe nodded. "I know. Both my great-grandparents were amazing. You wouldn't believe what Dante went through to get what he wanted. It makes me feel kind of stupid. Dante would never have let something like stage fright stop him from doing what he wanted to do."

"People get over stage fright, you know," Nyssa said

as she returned the mermaid's tail to the wardrobe. "I know you say you have it bad, but it doesn't have to be a life sentence."

"I know, I know." Chloe took a deep breath. "Actually, on that subject, I was kind of wondering—how late would be too late to put my name down for that talent show?"

Nyssa looked up. "You're changing your mind?"

"Don't get excited," said Chloe. "I'm not committing myself to anything yet. It's just, I've been thinking about how Dante never gave up. I don't know. I've been reading his memoir, exploring his house—maybe some of his determination is rubbing off on me."

"So do you still have your entry form?"

"I threw it away," Chloe said sheepishly.

"No problem," said Nyssa. "I can get you another one tonight."

"Wait—" Chloe threw up her hands. "You have to understand. Just talking about this makes me feel sick. It's like there's this *thing* inside me, waiting to pounce when I even *think* about performing."

"So do you want to do it or not?" asked Nyssa.

"I *want* to do it. I just need to take it in little steps."

Nyssa shrugged. "All right, I'll get the form then."

"Thanks," Chloe said, letting out her breath. "Guess I'll have to start doing some serious practicing."

"You'd better. You've only got a few weeks left. Sorry," Nyssa added when she saw the pained expression on Chloe's face. "Little steps. I won't say another word."

Chloe and Nyssa worked their way through the storage room and two other rooms next to it, but they didn't find the lock that went with Chloe's tiny key.

They were on their way downstairs shortly before suppertime when Nyssa came to a halt on the first-floor landing. "Lake's still there," she said as she peered at the painting of the carnival.

Chloe stepped forward to look. "The lake hasn't changed, but he's moved." She pointed at the snake charmer crouched beside a cage full of snakes. "And so has he," she said, moving her finger to the magician seated on a crate beside the snake charmer. "Plus the fiery balls he was juggling are gone."

"Are you sure?" said Nyssa. "It looks the same to me. I didn't memorize all the details."

Chloe shook her head in exasperation. "It's different, really! Can't you see that?"

"I don't know," said Nyssa. "Is it possible that you're getting the details confused with something you dreamed about?"

Chloe folded her arms across her chest. "I didn't dream it, and I'm not making this up. I know what I saw."

"Sorry, Chloe," Nyssa said with a shrug. "When you said the lake was different, that's all I really paid attention to. I promise I'll check it more carefully next time. Tomorrow, okay?"

Chloe made her way to the sitting room after dinner that evening. "This is for real," she told herself as she closed the door firmly behind her and took a seat at the piano.

She stretched her fingers and ran through her scales first. When she'd completed the scales, she played a passage from Debussy's *Clair de Lune* from memory. She worked at the passage until she was satisfied that her wrists and fingers were limber, and then she turned to the sheet music she'd discovered earlier inside the piano bench. Most of the music had proven to be too simple to hold her interest, but there were a few pieces that stood out from the rest. There was a Chopin nocturne and a handwritten arrangement called *The Ballad of Petticoat Joe* that had a number of challenging passages.

Chloe carefully arranged the pages of *Petticoat Joe* on the ledge in front of her. She tackled the piece in parts, playing first the right-hand part and then the left. Slowly, note by note, the piece began to take shape under her fingers. She tried playing it through with both hands, but it was a fast piece and the rhythm was tricky in a few sections. "It'll come," she told herself. She pushed a stray curl out of her eye and started again from the top.

Lying awake in bed later that night, Chloe thought about the story her great-aunts had shared with her. "Am I obsessed too?" Chloe asked herself. Dante had wanted the whole world to recognize him; she just wanted enough confidence to appear in front of an audience without humiliating herself. That wasn't so much to ask, was it?

"You're a perfectionist," her piano teacher had told her. "Aiming high is good, but don't set the bar so high that you can never be satisfied with yourself."

In the dark and silent bedroom, Chloe grimaced. She wasn't setting the bar very high this time. All she wanted was to get through the next recital without freezing up entirely. All she wanted was to survive it.

Outside on the landing, the grandfather clock struck the first hour of midnight. Chloe's thoughts turned to the painting of the carnival that hung beside the clock. "And what's *that* about? she whispered. She'd sounded like an idiot in front of Nyssa that afternoon, but the painting *had* changed, no matter what her friend thought.

Chloe felt a sudden overwhelming urge to check the painting before she fell asleep. She rose from her bed and crept down the hallway. A faint whispering sound made her pause at the foot of the stairs, but when she held her breath and strained to hear the sound again, it had stopped. Only the rhythmic ticking of the tall clock remained.

Chloe forced herself to continue up the stairs.

There was just enough moonlight coming through the windows on the second floor for Chloe to make out the rectangular shape of the painting on the landing. It was too dark to see details, but as she leaned in, she saw the silhouettes of tall trees—a forest that hadn't been there the last time she looked. And the sky…it was almost glowing with—Chloe drew her breath in sharply. There were tiny sparkling *stars* all over the painted sky. This morning the painting had displayed a daylight scene. Now it was unquestionably night.

Chapter Nine

"It's changed," Chloe insisted as she led Nyssa up to the landing the next morning. "I'm not imagining things, I'm not making it up. The painting is totally different. Just look!"

Nyssa stared at the painting, her eyebrows lifted. "Weird. It's got to be a different painting." She shook her head. "All I can say is that someone sure is going to a lot of trouble to mess with your head."

"I don't get it," said Chloe. "Who would want to do that? And why—what's the point?"

Nyssa shrugged. "My dad said he's heard your great-aunts were real practical jokers when they were younger. Bess especially."

"*Bess*?" said Chloe. "Maybe sixty or seventy years ago, but now? I don't think so. Even if she had a reason to, there's no way she could lift a painting this size off the wall."

"Maybe your aunts' housekeeper is in on it. Or maybe the housekeeper is doing it all by herself."

"Abigail?" said Chloe. "Okay, what's *her* motive supposed to be?"

"Maybe she's bored," Nyssa said. "Maybe it's a prank she plays on every houseguest. You did say she was hinting about weird stuff going on in this house."

Chloe shook her head. "It's not Abigail."

"How do you know it's not her?" Nyssa asked. "Have you got a webcam hidden in her room?"

"I just don't believe it's her."

"C'mon, Chloe," said Nyssa. "It's like you *want* this painting to be magic."

"Close your eyes," said Chloe.

"What?"

"Just close your eyes. There *is* something going on in this house. If you close your eyes and stay quiet, you can feel it. It's like there are strange vibrations in the air."

"Oooh, I think I can feel them," said Nyssa, pretending to shiver.

Chloe opened her eyes and punched her friend lightly in the shoulder. "I'm serious."

"Ouch," said Nyssa. "I'm serious too, Chloe. I'm seriously concerned that you seem to have a thing about ghosts and magic paintings."

"So what if I do believe in them? It's not like anyone has proved they don't exist."

"That's not true," said Nyssa. "There's a rational explanation for every single supernatural phenomenon that's ever been investigated by real scientists. Sometimes they're products of weather or geography, but mostly they're hoaxes. I'm just finishing a book about Harry Houdini. Do you have any idea how much time and energy he spent going after all the spiritualists who were around back then?"

"Spiritualists?"

Nyssa nodded. "You know, mediums. People who claimed they could talk to the dead and make tables levitate and all that stuff. The spirit cabinet trick is a classic example. That's the one where the magician is gagged and tied up tight inside a narrow wooden wardrobe-thing."

"I know the one you mean," said Chloe. "I read about it in Dante's memoir."

"Right. Well, when a spiritualist performed that trick, people actually believed they saw a ghost's hands and heard spirits knocking and playing musical instruments. Of course it was really the man inside doing everything. He didn't have any supernatural powers—he was just very good at slipping in and out of the ropes that were supposed to be securing him. It was what he knew about knots, not spirits, that counted."

"And your point is?" said Chloe.

"My point is that everything they did was a hoax. They were scam artists, going after people's money."

"No one's going after my money here," Chloe pointed out. "Not that I have any."

"I'm just saying there has to be an explanation for this painting. How about this? Maybe someone's trying to distract you from this stage fright thing you've been going through."

"That is truly the lamest explanation you've come up with so far," Chloe said as she turned away from the painting.

Nyssa followed Chloe back down the stairs. "So how *is* the stage fright thing going? Have you started practicing for the talent show yet?"

"*Yes*, I've been practicing. I practiced for three hours last night. And I practiced for an hour before you showed up, and I'll practice again when you're gone, thank you very much."

"Don't let me keep you then," Nyssa said cheerfully as they reached the front door.

"Seriously," Chloe said, taking a deep breath. "In a few days I'd like to do a mini-recital for you and my aunts and Abigail."

"Really?" asked Nyssa. "You're that close?"

"I will be—I hope." Chloe bit down on her lip. "Here's how I'm looking at it—I'll either get through it and be fine, or I'll have a heart attack and die. In which case it will all be over and I won't have to do the talent show."

"Cool. So can I bring my dad's digital camcorder?"

Chloe smiled at her friend. "If you don't mind me feeding it to you, you can."

"All right," Nyssa said, putting her hands up. "I'll come unarmed."

A few afternoons later, Chloe's guests assembled in the sitting room.

"This is quite an honor," Kitty said as she took a seat in one of the two armchairs. Bess was already seated in the other chair. Abigail and Nyssa were perched on the chintz-covered love seat across from the elderly sisters. All four faces were turned toward Chloe.

Chloe took a deep breath and tried to will her pounding heart to slow down. "Tide in, tide out," she whispered to herself. She inhaled and exhaled slowly. Then she lifted her hands to her thighs to wipe her sweaty palms on her shorts. Her voice broke on the first word of her introduction, and she had to clear her throat and start again. "My first piece is one I found inside the piano bench. It's called *The Ballad of Petticoat Joe.*"

Kitty clapped her hands. "That's one of my favorites! I haven't heard it for decades. It was arranged by a friend of ours who used to play at St. Mark's, you know. The rhythm's a bit tricky, as I recall."

Chloe nodded weakly. "Well," she breathed, "here goes."

The first notes sounded awkward to Chloe. Her arms felt like wood. "I'm sorry. I messed that up," Chloe said as she came to an abrupt stop just seconds after she'd started.

"It was sounding good to me," said Abigail.

Kitty waved her hand in the air. "Just start over, dear. We don't mind."

Chloe had to fight to catch her breath again. Her stomach was churning, but she ignored it and raised her hands to the keyboard. She started again, forcing her fingers to travel across the keys and her eyes to find the notes written on the pages in front of her. She was almost halfway through *Petticoat Joe* before the music began to feel natural. Gradually her body relaxed and she grew more confident. By the final page, Chloe's fingers were flying.

When she finished, her small audience broke into applause immediately. "That was *wonderful*," Kitty cried, her hands clasped in delight.

"Bravo!" said Abigail. Even Bess was nodding.

"You *have* to play at the festival," said Nyssa. "That's *exactly* what the judges are looking for."

Chloe's body was still tense, and her face was hot. "I'm not finished yet," she said anxiously. "I still have two pieces to get through."

Kitty raised her hands for silence. "All right. We'll save our adulation for the end."

With the first piece out of the way, the remaining pieces were a little less agonizing. Chloe continued her short program with a ragtime melody she'd modified called *Sticks and Bones*. She finished with her favorite piece, Chopin's Nocturne in F-sharp Major.

"That was very impressive," Bess said with a nod of her chin when the clapping had subsided.

Abigail's eyes were wide behind her glasses. "Brilliant, just brilliant."

"Thanks," Chloe murmured, trembling and smiling at the same time.

"I did it—I survived!" Chloe said to Nyssa afterward, when the others were gone.

"You didn't just survive, you were awesome!" said Nyssa. She held out a piece of paper. "There's no way I'm letting you out of this room until you've filled out this entry form. You *have* to do the talent show."

"Look at my hands," said Chloe. "Look how much

they're shaking. And that's just from playing in front of four people!"

"You can do it, you *know* you can."

"But the show's just a few days away now!"

"Exactly," said Nyssa. "My dad's sending the program to the printer tomorrow morning." She waved the entry form in the air. "This is your last chance."

Chloe shook her head vigorously. "I can't. There's no way I'd be ready."

"C'mon, you're ready now! Just fill it out, okay? You can always drop out later if you have to."

"Has anyone ever told you how pushy you are?" Chloe asked as Nyssa held the paper directly in front of her face.

"Just take it."

Chloe stared at her friend for a moment before grabbing the paper out of her hand. "All right. I'm taking it. But I'm not committing to anything. If I have to back out at the last minute, I will. Deal?"

"Deal," said Nyssa.

Chapter Ten

"I think I'll do some more exploring upstairs this evening," Chloe told her great-aunts after supper.

"Good idea," said Kitty. "You could use a break from that piano. You've been practicing so much lately, you must have calluses on your fingers."

Chloe made her way up to the third floor and let herself into what at one time must have been the master bedroom. It was a spacious room with large shuttered windows and high ceilings, dominated by a giant canopied bed.

Chloe examined every item in the room, removing drawers and checking for secret compartments in each piece of furniture. She'd just removed some quilts from a large wooden chest next to the bed when she discovered the chest had a false bottom. She pushed at the boards, and then she tried to pry up a loose board with her fingernails. When she couldn't quite lift it, she reached for a silver letter opener on a nearby desk and inserted it into the crack. Carefully she pulled one end of the board up, holding it just high enough so that she could squeeze her free hand through the gap.

At first Chloe felt nothing, but as she moved her hand around the hidden space, her fingers made contact with the curled edges of a piece of paper. Chloe withdrew the document carefully. It was a letter from Magdala to Dante, dated February 13, 1918.

My Dear Dante,

I am not sure why I am writing to you, since I have nowhere to send a letter. Perhaps it is because the baby that I am carrying is almost due. I cannot speak with you, to remind you of our child, so instead I set my words down on this page.

You have been missing for two months now. Though the officers assigned to your case are sympathetic to our family's plight, their official investigation has all but come to a close. I cannot fault them. They followed every lead, no matter how unlikely, but in the end they learned nothing new.

The police released your few things to me yesterday: the posters, the painting of the carnival and the rosewood box. I hung the painting on the first-floor landing, but I didn't know what to do with Monsieur Lucien's box. I was going to throw it in the fire, but when I took it in my hands I found that I could not destroy it. If the box is indeed linked with your disappearance, as I believe in my heart, then it remains my only connection to you, my only hope, dark as that hope might be. And so, instead of burning the box, I have hidden it away in the secret attic. Now I can only pray that its evil influence will remain contained, that its taint will not spread through this house.

Do you think of us wherever you are, Dante? Every day the girls ask where you are and when you will return. As they kneel beside their beds at night, I hear them praying, begging God to keep you safe, to bring you home. Though my own faith has almost disappeared, I can never resist making a silent appeal of my own.

Where did you go, Dante? Where did your terrible ambition take you?

Chloe's heart was beating furiously as she let her great-grandmother's letter fall to the floor. In the failing light, her hand found the tiny golden key that hung at her throat. The rosewood wishing box had not been destroyed. It was hidden in this very house. It was waiting for her; Chloe could feel it.

Chloe slept fitfully that night. She rose at dawn the next morning, grabbed a quick bowl of cereal before anyone else was up and rushed upstairs to begin hunting for the secret attic.

She started in the master bedroom. When she spied a trapdoor in the ceiling of an alcove off the main room, she was sure her search was over. But the enclosed space at the top of the turret was empty and led nowhere.

From the bedroom, Chloe moved down the hall to a

storage room crammed with magic paraphernalia. She made a mental note to tell Nyssa about it. Chloe would have liked to spend some time examining her great-grandfather's bits and pieces, but her eagerness to find the hidden attic kept her focused. She inspected every square inch of the floor, ceiling and walls, opening wardrobes and chests, tapping everywhere for false bottoms or panels.

When she was finished with the storage room, Chloe moved on to the small library next door. Leather-bound books in tall shelves covered all four walls of the room. A spiral staircase led to a book-filled loft. Chloe pushed and pulled a few sections of each bookcase experimentally. Then she began removing books systematically, shelf by shelf, as she'd done in the nursery downstairs. She'd explored most of one wall in this fashion before she was called down to lunch.

Chloe returned to the library in the afternoon, completing her circuit of the first level and starting up the spiral stairs to the loft. She had more luck on the second floor of the library. A revolving door built into one of the bookcases led her to a tiny hidden alcove and out onto a narrow balcony. But like the space above the turret in the master bedroom, both the alcove and the balcony were empty.

"It's so frustrating," Chloe told Nyssa as the two girls sat together on the front steps after lunch the next day. "Dante's box is in this house somewhere. I just can't find it."

"Tell me you aren't taking the story of the wishing box seriously," said Nyssa. "Remember, magicians exaggerate everything. It's part of their mystique; they build up a larger-than-life history for themselves."

"But I didn't read about it in Dante's memoir," Chloe argued. "My aunts told me about the wishing box."

"Don't you think they might have embellished the facts a little to make the family history more interesting?"

"Kitty might embellish things, but Bess wouldn't. Besides, you've read Magdala's letter. She not only mentioned the box; she believed it had something to do with Dante's disappearance."

"Right," said Nyssa. "*I can only pray that its evil influence will remain contained, that its taint will not spread through this house.*" She rolled her eyes. "C'mon, Chloe. It sounds like a line from a really sappy ghost story. People don't talk like that in real life."

"Whatever," Chloe said stubbornly, folding her arms across her chest. "But I'm *not* going to stop looking for the secret attic or the rosewood box."

"Don't you have more important things to worry about right now, like getting ready for the show? It's just a few days away."

"I'm still practicing," said Chloe. "I'm capable of doing both, you know. Preparing for the show *and* searching the house."

"All right, all right," said Nyssa. "So where have you looked so far?"

"Everywhere," Chloe sighed. "I've searched every room in the house."

"Have you looked for it outside the house?"

Chloe stared at her friend. A smile spread slowly across her face.

"What?" said Nyssa.

"That's it! It's that simple! Three generations of McBrides have already explored the house. If the secret attic could be reached from the inside, someone would have found it already. The entrance to Magdala's attic must be on the outside!"

Nyssa raised her eyebrows. "So what are we waiting for?"

Exploring the outside of the old Victorian mansion was not a simple task. Nyssa and Chloe made a circuit of the building at ground level first, but it was clear they'd have to climb considerably higher if they wanted to find an exterior entrance to a hidden attic.

"Do your great-aunts have a ladder?" Nyssa asked.

"I don't know. I haven't seen one anywhere," said Chloe. "But there's a perfectly good trellis on the other side of this lilac bush."

Nyssa squeezed in after Chloe and gave the ivy-covered trellis an experimental tug. "You think it will hold us?"

"It's mostly solid. We'll go one at a time. I'll go first," said Chloe. She found a handhold and began pulling herself up.

"How is it?" Nyssa asked from below.

"Stable, so far. There's a ledge here. If I can just get my leg over—"

"Hey, be careful. I'm the one who's going to have to explain this to your aunts if you fall."

"Don't worry, I made it," Chloe called back. "I'm on the first roof."

"I'm right behind you."

Climbing from the small first-floor overhang to the next level proved to be even more challenging. Chloe had to hang on to a series of window ledges and old pipes to get to the top of the second story. Nyssa followed a few moves behind. From the second story, the roofline became more complicated and therefore easier to climb.

"There's quite a view from up here," Nyssa said shakily as she swung her leg over the railing of a third-story balcony after Chloe.

"Look what I found!" said Chloe. "There's a ladder on the wall just on the other side of this shutter. I never would have noticed it if we hadn't climbed out here. This could be it, the entrance to Magdala's secret attic!"

"Be careful," Nyssa cautioned as Chloe reached across the shutter for the nearest ladder rung. With her right hand gripping the bottom of the ladder, Chloe climbed back up onto the ledge of the balcony. From there she was able to reach for the next rung with her left hand. She wedged her feet against the side of the shutters and began climbing.

"I've found something," Chloe called down when she'd reached the fifth rung. "There's a small window hidden under the roof overhang."

"What do you see?"

"Not much," Chloe said as she tried to peer in. "The glass is filthy. I'm going to try to open it." She turned the window's exterior latch and gently pulled the handle on the side of the frame. It refused to budge. She tightened the grip of her left hand on the ladder and pulled the handle harder with her right hand. After a few seconds of continuous tugging, the window frame gave a reluctant creak and slowly swung out. "I've got it open," Chloe called down, her heart pounding. "I'm going in."

The window opening was small, but Chloe was able to wriggle through without getting stuck. As her eyes grew accustomed to the dim light, she saw that she was crouched in a tiny chamber. There was a dusty pile in the far corner of the dark space. "I've found something," she called out the window, unable to keep the excitement from her voice.

"What?"

"Just a second. It's hard to see in here." Chloe knelt on the plank floor. "There's a wooden box and some papers. Can you climb up partway so I can pass them out to you?"

Chloe had just made her way back down the ladder to the balcony when Abigail's head appeared in a window one story below them, startling both girls.

"Didn't mean to scare you," said the housekeeper. "I heard some thumping and banging as I was dusting in here. Weren't you going to the beach this afternoon? Anyway, I'm glad I found you. If you call your mother right away, Nyssa, you'll save her a trip down to the lake to search for you. Your grandparents have just arrived."

"Great timing," Nyssa muttered when Abigail had pulled her head back in. "Sorry—they weren't supposed to be here until dinnertime."

"You don't have to go right away, do you?" Chloe asked. "This could be it—this could be Dante's rosewood box!"

Nyssa nodded reluctantly. "I know, but I'd better go. My grandparents just flew back from a trek in New Zealand. They're on their way home to Thunder Bay. Sorry. You'll have to check it out without me."

Chloe walked Nyssa downstairs and took the wooden box and the papers to the back garden. She set everything down on one of the stone benches in the clearing, sat down beside the pile and took a deep breath.

The stack of papers she'd rescued was a collection of letters from Dante to Magdala. Chloe riffled through them briefly before setting them aside. Her palms damp, she reached for the small, ornately carved, dark wooden box. She wiped the lid carefully with the hem of her T-shirt, admiring the intricate vines and exotic fruits that appeared from underneath layers of dust. She lifted the box to study it more closely and caught the faint but unmistakable scent of roses.

The box was locked. Somehow Chloe knew that her key would be a match even before she removed it from around her neck and tried it in the keyhole. The key turned without any trouble, and the latch was released. She paused to wipe her hands on her shorts, and then she slowly lifted the lid. The box was empty.

Chloe put the box down on the bench and considered her next move. What she wanted to do was write down a wish, place it in the box and see what happened. But if Magdala was right, the box was dangerous. Chloe removed the tiny key from the box and clutched it in her fist. A few minutes passed as she wrestled with her choices. I have to do it, she told herself silently. I have to see if it's real.

She ran back to the house for some paper and a pen. When she returned, she scribbled down the first wish that came into her head, pushed the folded paper inside the box, closed the lid and quickly inserted the key. "There," she said aloud to break the silence that hung heavily over the clearing. "It's done."

Five minutes passed and nothing happened. "This is ridiculous," Chloe told herself at last. She gathered together the box and Dante's letters and got up.

"Chloe!" Abigail called out as the girl came through the back door. "I was just about to go looking for you."

Chloe clutched the bundle in her arms self-consciously. "What is it?"

The housekeeper gave a short laugh and nodded toward the kitchen. "Come see."

As Chloe entered the kitchen behind Abigail, a man was just hanging up the phone that hung by the refrigerator. "Like I was saying," the man said to the housekeeper, "you might as well fill up your freezer. The tow truck won't be here for at least another forty-five minutes, according to the dispatcher. On a hot day like this, it's all going to melt if it stays where it is."

"Mr. Shambhu's ice-cream truck just broke down on the road right in front of the house," Abigail explained to Chloe.

"Strangest thing," the man said, scratching the back of his head. "The truck engine, the generator for my freezers, and my cell phone all went dead at the same time. I guess my bad luck is your good luck."

"Are you sure about this?" said Abigail. "We could return everything to your truck after it's been repaired."

Mr. Shambhu waved his hand. "Don't worry about it. My truck could be in the shop for a while."

"Well, thank you. It's very generous of you." Abigail turned back to Chloe. "There you go. Give Mr. Shambhu a hand, and you and Nyssa will have all the ice-cream bars and Popsicles you can eat for the rest of your visit."

Chloe shut her mouth and swallowed hard. "Could you give me a minute?" she mumbled. She was already backing up, making her way to the end of the hall where she'd left the rosewood box. With trembling fingers she unlocked the box and removed a slip of paper. She unfolded the paper and read the words she'd scribbled less than half an hour earlier: *I wish for all the ice cream I can eat.*

Chapter Eleven

"It was a totally lame thing to wish for, I know," Chloe told Nyssa as they sat on the front steps the next morning. "I just wrote down the first thing that popped into my head. I thought it was pretty safe."

"And? Wait, don't tell me," said Nyssa. "Let me use my psychic powers. Abigail went shopping and came back with a few pints of Häagen-Dazs."

"Hold your skepticism for a minute. It wasn't like that at all." Chloe told her friend the whole story, from writing down her wish to Mr. Shambhu's multiple breakdowns in front of the house.

"It's a coincidence, Chloe," Nyssa insisted. "Weird, but still a coincidence."

"How can you say that?" Chloe shook her head in frustration. "I make a wish, and Mr. Shambhu's truck breaks down, his generator dies and his cell phone battery goes dead, all in the space of less than half an hour, right in front of this house. What are the odds?"

Nyssa shrugged. "It's a long shot, but it isn't impossible. What *is* impossible is a box that grants wishes. Please tell me you don't believe in fairy tales."

"Dante believed the box's powers were real. And Magdala was afraid of Monsieur Lucien because she believed in its powers too."

Nyssa just shook her head. "So what are you going to do with this 'magic' box?"

"Make another wish, of course. A better one this time. I'll have to think about it."

Nyssa rose to her feet. "Well, while you're thinking about it, why don't you get on the back of my bike and I'll double you down to the lake."

The two friends were making their way back from the beach at lunchtime when a man in dark sunglasses suddenly stepped onto the bike path directly in front of them. Nyssa tried to swerve, but with Chloe's added weight on the back she lost control. The bike went down.

"I'm sorry," the man said as Nyssa and Chloe untangled themselves from each other and the bike. "I seem to have walked into your path."

"No problem," Nyssa replied. "You okay, Chloe?"

Chloe brushed some loose gravel from her knees. "I'm fine. Just a few scratches."

"Chloe," the man repeated, pronouncing the name carefully. "You must be Katherine and Elizabeth's niece."

Chloe looked up at the dark-haired stranger. He was

about her father's age, but at least half a foot taller. He was dressed rather formally for a summer stroll in the park, in a dark suit and tie.

"Lucas Dromnel," he said as he extended his right hand. "I just moved into a suite in the house next door to your great-aunts."

Chloe shook the offered hand. Mr. Dromnel's skin was cool to the touch, but his grip was firm.

"I'm Nyssa," Nyssa said, thrusting out her own hand. "I live around the corner."

Lucas Dromnel shook Nyssa's hand as well. "A pleasure to meet you both," he said with a smile. "I'm sure we'll be bumping into each other again."

"*He* was creepy," Chloe said with a shudder when they were safely out of earshot. "Did you see the way he was staring?"

"How could you tell he was staring through those dark sunglasses?" Nyssa asked.

"'Cause I could feel his eyes on me—couldn't you? And what was up with the dark suit?"

"I don't know. Maybe he's an insurance salesman or a funeral director or something."

"Or maybe he's in the Mafia," Chloe suggested as they turned off the path and prepared to cross St. Mark's Street.

Nyssa raised an eyebrow. "The Mafia?"

"I don't know," said Chloe. "I just didn't trust him."

"All right then. Moving along to other fantastical subjects," Nyssa said as they came to a stop by Chloe's front gate, "have you decided on your next wish?"

Chloe nodded. "I've got something in mind. It's not

world peace or anything, but it's better than a supply of ice-cream bars."

"Yeah? What?"

"I'll tell you after lunch," said Chloe. "Are you staying?"

"Can't. I promised my mom I'd be home in twenty minutes." Nyssa made a face. "I've got a dress fitting. I'm a bridesmaid at my cousin's wedding at the end of August, which means I have to wear this hideous purple sack."

"All right," said Chloe. "Meet me back here as soon as you're done. We'll see who's right about the wishing box."

Chloe excused herself from the table immediately after lunch and returned to her room. She took a seat on her bed, facing the rosewood box. "Okay," she whispered. "Let's get it right this time." Carefully she wrote out her wish. She read it over, placed the note inside the box, closed the lid and turned the tiny key. She left the box on the desk beside her bed and went out to the veranda.

Chloe had just sat down on the top step when she saw Nyssa come racing around the corner, two houses down. "Hey," Nyssa called out, lifting one hand off the handlebars to wave. A blue van suddenly pulled out of a driveway into Nyssa's path.

"Nyssa!" Chloe yelled.

The warning came too late. As Chloe watched in horror, Nyssa's bicycle ran straight into the van, and Nyssa flew over the windshield. She came down with a sickening thud.

Chloe raced onto the road. "Nyssa!" she screamed again. "Nyssa!"

The street was suddenly full of people. "Don't touch her," warned a man who'd been jogging on the path across the road. "We don't want to injure her spine."

"I've called nine-one-one," said another man with a cell phone in his hand. "An ambulance will be here any minute."

"Oh my god, oh my god," moaned the woman whose van Nyssa had hit. "I didn't see her coming!"

"Nyssa," Chloe cried, standing helplessly a few feet away.

Then someone was dragging her away, and she could hear Abigail's soothing voice in her ear. "It's okay, Chloe. Listen, the ambulance is almost here. They'll take good care of her. She'll be all right."

Chloe let herself be led back up to the house, where her great-aunts waited anxiously on the veranda. "Oh, how horrible, my dear," Kitty said as she gathered the numb girl into her arms. "Look, the paramedics are here already. Nyssa will be all right now, don't you worry."

Chloe tried to break away from her great-aunt's embrace. "I have to see her!"

"No, Chloe," Bess said firmly. "You'd only be in the way. I phoned Nyssa's mother, and she's on her way to meet Nyssa at the hospital. She'll call as soon as she has news."

Kitty gave Chloe another squeeze. "Nyssa's going to be all right, you'll see. Now come inside and lie down. You're in shock."

After six hours that felt more like six weeks, the phone finally rang. "Hello?" Chloe said breathlessly.

"Hey, Chloe."

"Nyssa?"

"Who else?"

Chloe felt tears trickle down her cheeks. "Oh, Nyssa!"

"C'mon, don't get all teary on me. I'm fine. Aside from a concussion, a few cracked ribs and a broken radius, that is."

"A broken what?"

"My right arm."

Chloe's fingers were white around the phone. "Oh, Nyssa—I was so scared!"

"They want to observe me for a little while. The doctor I saw in emergency said I would have split my head open if it wasn't for my bike helmet. You should see it."

"Your bike's all right," Chloe said hoarsely. "At least, that's what the woman whose van you collided with told Abigail. Not a scratch."

"So I heard. I asked my dad to drop my bike off at your aunts' house. My mom doesn't want me riding with a cast on my arm. You might as well get some use out of it."

Chloe felt as if a large marble had suddenly wedged itself inside her throat. "No," she whispered.

"Chloe? Are you okay?"

Chloe swallowed, her breath stuck somewhere in her chest. "Oh, Nyssa," she choked out. "I'm so sorry."

"For what?" Nyssa asked. "I'm the one who wasn't watching where I was going."

"No, you don't understand!"

"Understand *what*? Sorry, Chloe, I have to go. The nurse has just come in to check me over again. I'll call you later if I can."

"Wait, I need to tell you—" Chloe said. But it was too late. Nyssa had already hung up.

Chloe tried to practice the piano in the sitting room, but her heart wasn't in it. After playing a few scales, she abandoned the piano and returned to her room. She forced her eyes past the rosewood box on her desk to the stack of letters beside it. She picked up the letters and carried them through the front of the house to the veranda.

Kitty, Bess and Abigail were seated at the wicker table, sipping iced tea. They invited Chloe to join them, but she declined. She sat on the steps instead and began to read the first letter in her pile. It was a letter from Dante to Magdala, dated July 14, 1917, less than two weeks after Magdala had abandoned the carnival with her daughters and returned to Little Venice.

Dear Maggie,

I trust that you and the girls had a safe journey and are now comfortably settled in the house. I am sorry that you feel unable to stay with the carnival while Monsieur Lucien is present. But as I respected your decision to return home with the twins, I hope you understand my decision to keep Lucien with the carnival.

I can't tell you how helpful he has been. We are drawing record audiences to every performance. Even without active promotion, the news of my new "Phoenix" act precedes us like wildfire. People are willing to pay over and over again to see this amazing spectacle. If that isn't enough, Lucien says that he will teach me to perform even greater illusions before the season is over.

This is it, Maggie. I can feel it. With Lucien's help I am finally going to achieve the kind of success that I have dreamed of for so many years. I will be the world's greatest magician!

Chloe had just moved Dante's first letter to the bottom of the pile when a familiar male voice called up from the sidewalk. "Good evening, ladies."

"Good evening, Mr. Dromnel," Kitty called back.

"Fine weather we're having," Lucas Dromnel said. He was still wearing sunglasses, even though the sun was low on the horizon.

"Weather's holding for the moment," Bess said. "But I can feel a storm brewing."

Mr. Dromnel turned his face toward the cloudless sky. "You could be right. I believe I can smell a little lightning in the air myself."

Abigail shuddered girlishly. "I've never liked thunderstorms. They're so terribly destructive."

"But that's what makes them so exciting, don't you think? What would life be without a little danger now and then?" said Mr. Dromnel. He excused himself with a nod of his head and continued up the sidewalk to the house next door.

"There's something familiar about our new neighbor," Kitty said once he'd disappeared behind some shrubbery. "I can't quite put my finger on it. Ah well. There are so many faces rattling around in this old brain, it's no wonder they're all beginning to blend together."

When it was time to go to bed, Chloe carried her great-grandfather's letters inside with her. Through the summer and into the fall of 1917, Dante's letters were almost interchangeable. Dante missed his wife and children, but the excitement of seeing his ambitions realized outweighed anything else. Then in late November, Dante's mood shifted abruptly.

> *Dear Maggie,*
>
> *I had a troubling conversation with Lucien this morning at breakfast. In my excitement at having been interviewed by a journalist from the* Chicago Tribune *yesterday evening, I told Lucien that his wishing box had proved its worth many times over and that I was ready to settle on a price. He just stared at me for a moment, with a half-smile on his lips. Then, to my surprise, he said that I had been paying his price all along.*
>
> *At first I didn't understand. Or maybe it would be more honest to say I pretended not to understand. But as I stared back into Lucien's dark eyes, I began to see clearly what I had chosen not to see before. For every wish I made, there was a terrible consequence that I'd refused to acknowledge. You saw some of the results yourself: I wished for gold and received someone else's stolen coins; I wished for a fiery new illusion and someone else was consumed by real flames. As my mind traveled back through the list of crimes and misfortunes that paralleled my wishes, I became increasingly ashamed and horrified. Of course*

I ordered Lucien to take his evil box and leave at once. If only I'd listened to your concerns earlier!"

As Chloe read the final paragraph of Dante's letter, she felt a sharp pain in the pit of her stomach. It all suddenly made sense. "Nyssa," she whispered, "my stupid wish could have killed you!"

There was one final unread letter in the pile. Chloe smoothed it out carefully.

Dear Maggie,

Please try to understand what I am about to tell you. I know I wrote just yesterday to say that I was sending Lucien away, but after speaking with him again last night, I have reconsidered.

The truth is, everything in life has a price. And while it may not seem just, the person who pays the price is not necessarily the person who reaps the reward. As Lucien reminded me, generals win their battles at the expense of their foot soldiers, and wealthy men earn their money on the backs of their laborers. Harsh as that might sound, it's the way the world works.

What I'm trying to say is that Lucien has made me an offer that I cannot refuse. He packed his belongings last night as I'd asked him to, but before leaving he put the rosewood box in my hands one final time. Something strange happened to me as I held the box. I could hear Lucien speaking, but his voice seemed to come from a great distance. "Everything you want is in that box," he said. "Your deepest ambitions, everything you've ever dreamed of. You could be the greatest magician the world has ever seen. All you have to do is ask."

If only you could have seen the images that flickered through my mind at that moment, Maggie. If you could have heard the distant music and smelled the intoxicating scent rising from the box in my hands, I know you would understand my decision. I have waited my whole adult life for this chance. I can't let it slip away now, no matter what the price.

If there was any hesitation left in my mind, it evaporated when Lucien told me that he intended to extend the offer of one wish to each of the other performers in the carnival. They have been such loyal companions for so many years—and now they get to share in my good fortune as well!

I need you to understand. After I have made this final wish, I promise that I will never use the rosewood box again. I won't need to, once I'm the world's greatest magician. Just think what that honor will mean for us, Maggie! Everything that we've ever dreamed of, wished for, imagined—it will all be ours!

Chloe let her great-grandfather's letter fall onto the bed. She looked at the rosewood box on her desk with a mixture of fear and revulsion. It would be impossible to sleep with the box sitting just a few feet away. She got out of bed and forced herself to pick the box up. Holding it out at arm's length, Chloe left her room and tiptoed down the dark hallway to the staircase at the center of the house.

The ticking of the clock on the first landing sounded

ominously loud. Chloe tried not to think about the painting hanging beside it in the shadows. She climbed up through the dark house, through the library on the third floor and up the spiral stairs to the loft. Holding the wooden box in front of her, she moved quickly out onto the tiny balcony. With her free hand, she felt carefully around the shutter for the first rung of the exterior ladder. Her heart was beating furiously as she began to climb in the moonlight, over the railing and up the short ladder to Magdala's secret attic. She had to wedge the rosewood box between her stomach and the ladder to free up a hand to open the window. When it was open, Chloe took the box and shoved it as far as she could into the dark space.

Chapter Twelve

"You look worse than me, if that's possible," Nyssa said to Chloe the next morning. Nyssa was half lying, half sitting in a raised hospital bed. A white cast encased her right forearm.

Chloe sat down in the chair beside Nyssa's bed. "Bad dreams—don't ask."

"Worried about the show tomorrow night?"

"It's not that," Chloe said, staring down at her fingernails. "Although with everything that's happened, you can't really expect that I'd be up for the talent show."

"What do you mean?" Nyssa struggled to sit up further. "Don't tell me you're bailing on me. Your name is on the program and everything!"

"Hey," Chloe said, looking up quickly. "I told you when I filled out the entry form that I was reserving the right to back out whenever I wanted to. Anyway, your name is on the program too, and you aren't going to be there!"

"Believe me, if there was any way I could be there, I would be."

"But you *can't*," said Chloe, feeling her face flush. "And if you can't, I'm not going to do the show either."

Nyssa shook her head from side to side. "No way. You can't use my accident as an excuse to pull out now. You're prepared, Chloe. You have a real chance!"

"*You* had a chance before I made my stupid wish," Chloe said angrily. She let her eyes rest briefly on Nyssa's cast, and then she raised them to her friend's face again. "It's my fault you're lying here."

"How on earth do you figure this is your fault?"

"Because it is," Chloe insisted, drawing herself up in the chair. "You know the wish I was going to make yesterday at lunchtime? I made it. I wished for a bike just like yours. And then you collided with Mrs. Larsen's minivan and ended up here, and I ended up with a bike *just like yours*. Your bike! Don't you get it?"

Nyssa's eyes went wide. "You wished for a bike just like mine?" She closed her eyes and remained silent for the space of a few breaths. Then she shook her head. "No, Chloe. That's just crazy. It was another coincidence, that's all it was."

"It wasn't a coincidence!" Chloe insisted. "It's the way the rosewood box works. I read it in Dante's letters."

"Where's the box now?"

"Back in the secret attic. I put it there last night."

Nyssa nodded. "Good. You should leave it there."

"Finally you believe me," said Chloe.

"I don't believe the box is magic, but I do believe the *idea* of it is dangerous. Look how messed up you are right now. Forget about it. Focus on getting ready for the show."

"I told you, I don't want to do the show."

Nyssa stared into her friend's face for a few seconds before sighing. "Whatever else Dante was, he wasn't a coward."

"Are you calling me a coward?" Chloe said angrily.

"Well what do you call what you're doing?"

"I call it common sense, knowing my limits."

"My dad always says that the only limits you have are the ones you put on yourself," said Nyssa. "Anyway, I'm being released this afternoon. I'll be really disappointed if I don't see you when the curtain rises tomorrow. Especially now that I can't be in the show myself."

Chloe tried to outstare her friend. "That is so low!" she said after a few seconds. She folded her arms across her chest. "Fine. If it means so much to you, I'll do it."

Abigail was waiting in the hallway to drive Chloe back to her great-aunts' house. The center of town was packed, forcing Abigail to slow the car to a crawl as she navigated the narrow main street toward the bridge that led across the canal.

"Good turnout for the festival," Abigail said as she edged her hatchback past a line of parked cars on one side and a stream of pedestrians on the other. "Most of the festival's shows are already sold out."

"How about the junior talent show?" Chloe asked, feeling her stomach flutter.

"Oh, that's been sold out for weeks," Abigail said with a careless wave of her hand. "Good thing we got our tickets at the beginning of the summer. It's quite a famous event here, you know. It's launched a few careers. Young people send in their audition tapes six months in advance, just to get a spot on the program."

Chloe turned to stare at Abigail. "Audition tapes? I didn't send in an audition tape."

"Yes, well, you're the exception. Your great-aunts' word was enough to convince Nyssa's father. As the program director for the festival, he has pull."

The butterflies fluttering in Chloe's stomach had suddenly become giant birds of prey. "I didn't know this talent show was such a big deal," she said in a strained voice.

The housekeeper took her right hand off the steering wheel just long enough to pat Chloe's leg. "Don't worry. You'll do fine. You're a McBride, after all."

Chloe made her way to the piano in the sitting room immediately after lunch and began running through her scales. "Don't think," she told herself sternly as she adjusted the sheet music on the ledge. "Just play."

As much as she tried to block the talent show from her mind, thoughts of it kept creeping in. Chloe's fingers felt like lead. They fell clumsily on the keys. "I *know* this," she told herself angrily as she stumbled through the climactic passage of *The Ballad of Petticoat Joe*. She forced herself to slow down, to go through the music on the page note by note, measure by measure, until she had it right again. Her cheeks blazed even though she was alone.

"You can't do this," a voice in her head insisted. "You're going to crash."

"I have to do this," she whispered fiercely. "And I'm *not* going to crash."

She took a deep breath and started again.

Kitty laid her hand on Chloe's forearm as the girl pushed her chair back from the table after dinner that evening. "Where are you off to now, my dear?"

"Back to the piano," Chloe said, lifting her napkin from her lap with her free hand. "I've still got a few more hours to put in before I go to bed."

"Give yourself a little rest tonight," said Kitty. "You know your music already. Run through it again in the morning if you want to, but give yourself the evening off."

"But I'm not ready," Chloe insisted, her voice strained. "I sound terrible!"

"You sound much better than you think," Bess told her from the other side of the table. "You can't hear yourself objectively right now."

Kitty gave Chloe's arm another pat. "Take a break. It's the kindest thing you can do for yourself tonight."

Chloe let herself out through the back door. The sky was just visible through the leafy canopy above her. Clouds had gathered since the afternoon, obscuring the sun and blanketing the garden in shadow. The clearing at the center of the overgrown yard was still. Chloe listened intently as she stood beside one of the stone benches, but there was nothing, not the gentle drone of bees, not the soft burbling of the fountain, not even a whisper of wind.

"The calm before the storm," a quiet voice said behind her.

Chloe spun around. "Mr. Dromnel! What are you doing here?" she stammered, her hands flying to her chest.

The intruder stepped forward from the shadows at the edge of the clearing. "There's a rusted gate on my side of the wall. I pushed it open just to see what was on the other side, and I found myself in this charming garden."

Chloe took a step backward, but her sandal caught the edge of the bench, and she stumbled slightly.

"I'm sorry," Mr. Dromnel said, holding up his palms. "I didn't mean to alarm you. I imagine you have enough on your mind already, with tomorrow's show."

"How do you know about the show?"

Mr. Dromnel smiled. "Your great-aunts, of course. They're quite proud of you. Although they did mention that the show is causing you some anxiety."

"I'll be fine," said Chloe.

"Of course you will," said Mr. Dromnel. "The trembling, the sweating, the nausea—they all pass in the end, don't they?" There was a faint rumbling overhead, and he looked up. "It looks like the storm your aunt predicted is about to break over us. I suppose we'd both better return inside."

That was all the dismissal that Chloe needed. She was already on the path back to her great-aunts' house as the first drops began to fall.

"Good luck tomorrow," she heard Lucas Dromnel call from somewhere behind her. She didn't look back.

Chapter Thirteen

With a flash of lightning and a drumroll of thunder, the rain began to fall in earnest. Chloe was wet through to the skin by the time she reached the back door. She slipped her muddy sandals off before heading to her bedroom in search of dry clothes.

At the threshold of her room, Chloe came to an abrupt stop. There was just enough light coming through the window to illuminate the rosewood box on her desk. "No," she said, recoiling. "No!" She turned and stumbled down the hallway toward the light in the kitchen.

"What is it, Chloe?" Abigail asked, her hands suspended above the sink.

"There's a wooden box on my desk," Chloe said, her voice trembling. "It wasn't there this morning. Did you put it there?"

Abigail wiped her hands on her apron. "I haven't been anywhere near your room today. You'll have to ask your—"

But Chloe was already across the hall, moving toward the sitting room.

"Take a breath, dear," Kitty said when Chloe appeared, white-faced, in the doorway. "You look like you're about to collapse."

As if on cue, Chloe's legs crumpled. Kitty and Bess rose in alarm, but Chloe had already steadied herself against the doorframe. She let the two elderly women lead her to the love seat on the other side of the room.

"You're soaking wet," Kitty said when Chloe was seated. "We'll have to get you into something dry."

"I've brought a towel and a nightie," Abigail said from the doorway.

Three pairs of hands peeled Chloe's wet T-shirt and shorts from her shivering body and pulled the cotton nightgown over her head. There was a crash of thunder, and the lamp beside the love seat flickered and went out.

"There goes the electricity," said Abigail as she finished tucking a quilt in around Chloe's legs. "I'll get a fire going, and then I'll gather up some candles before it's too dark to see."

"Thank you, Abby," Chloe heard Kitty say. "Get a kettle of water to hang over the fire too. We'll make some chamomile tea, get something hot into her."

"What happened?" Bess asked when the housekeeper was gone.

Chloe shook her head, too disturbed to talk.

"I hope you're not coming down with something," Kitty said, leaning over to feel Chloe's forehead. "Poor dear. You've had a lot to deal with, haven't you?"

∼

The rosewood box was still sitting on the desk when Chloe returned to her room with a candle in her hand. The box seemed almost to be vibrating in the flickering candlelight, its shadow dancing on the far wall. Chloe forced herself to move toward the desk. She put her candle down, took a breath and reached for the box. It felt strangely soft and warm under her fingers, as if it had come alive. Chloe drew back her hands in horror.

She waited until her heart had slowed again before approaching the box a second time. With the aid of a pillow from her bed, she picked the box up and carried it quickly to the bedroom closet. Rain beat furiously against the windowpane as Chloe shoved the box into the darkest corner of the closet and slammed the door.

Outside on the landing, just audible over the storm, Chloe heard the grandfather clock chime ten times. She made it across the room and collapsed on her bed, drawing the covers around her trembling body. The clock had barely struck the quarter hour when Chloe slipped from consciousness into a vivid dream.

She was seated at a grand piano in the center of a large stage. There were lights trained on her, almost blinding in their intensity, but beyond the floodlights she could just make out tiers of seats—a huge auditorium that seemed to stretch on forever. The people in the auditorium cheered and called out her name as her fingers found the keys and the first bars of music rose from the piano.

After that, everything fell away, and she heard nothing but the music itself. She *was* the music, the notes rising and falling like the tides, blending together, coming apart, spinning, dancing. There was no sense of time in her dream. She played on without pause, measure after measure, her fingers flying, her heart soaring.

The music reached a final crescendo, and she became conscious of her body again. The audience was on its feet before she was even finished. She stood up and accepted the applause, let it pour over her and into her until she was close to bursting with it.

"You could have this," a soft voice whispered in her ear. "You could be the greatest concert pianist in the world."

She turned, startled. Lucas Dromnel stood beside her on the stage. "I don't need to be the best," she protested. "I just want to play."

"What you want is to be a concert pianist. That's what you told your friend Nyssa, remember? The world's great pianists don't play in church basements and town auditoriums—they play at Carnegie Hall. That's the secret you keep hidden, Chloe McBride. That's what really frightens you—that you'll never get there, that you don't have what it takes. That's why you shake and sweat and vomit before you perform."

The stage began to dissolve. Chloe heard Mr. Dromnel say something more, but the words were lost as she fought her way back up to the surface of consciousness.

In the darkness outside Chloe's bedroom, the clock on the landing chimed eleven times. Chloe was alert just long enough to register the clock, and then sleep pulled her under again.

This time the stage was unlit. She could smell her own nervous sweat and hear people whispering and muttering in the darkness around her. She reached out to orient herself and found the outlines of the piano bench and piano of her earlier dream. As she sat down on the bench, the floodlights came on. Blinded by the sudden brilliance, her hands flew to her eyes. The audience laughed cruelly. She looked down and saw that she was naked.

The piano keys glowed softly in front of her. As if she were a marionette controlled by invisible strings, her hands rose to the piano. But what her fingers produced was not music. It was noise, a discordant blend of notes that jarred and hurt her ears. There was no rhythm, no melody. There was only chaos, an angry child banging on an out-of-tune toy piano. Beyond the floodlights, the audience began to boo and hiss. The ugly sound rose around her like thunder, until there was no room for anything else. She wrenched her fingers from the keys.

The stage beneath her began to turn, and then suddenly it was not a stage but a carousel populated by wolves and wild dogs and other dark beasts. They were fixed in place on the carousel, and yet somehow they were alive, roaring and howling as the carousel spun faster and faster through the darkness. The bench she'd been sitting on had become a vicious hound. It yapped and growled as she clung to its black fur in terror.

Over the nightmarish music of the merry-go-round, over the roaring and howling of the angry dogs, she heard a new sound. It was a voice, calm and authoritative. She turned her head to the center of the carousel and saw Mr. Dromnel standing there, a half-smile on his lips. In his outstretched arms he held the rosewood box.

The music subsided, and the carousel slowed enough for Chloe to escape her growling mount and jump down to the ground. She was confronted by a dark forest. Her head was still spinning, but she forced her legs to carry her through the trees, away from the hideous merry-go-round. Behind her she heard Mr. Dromnel call her name, and she moved faster, over roots that tugged at her feet, through branches that caught at her limbs. She saw a light flicker through the underbrush off to the right and veered toward it. As she drew closer, she saw that the light was a bonfire at the center of a clearing. Even by firelight, she recognized the semicircle of tents that surrounded the fire. She hesitated on the edge of the clearing for just a moment before a shadowy figure emerged from the nearest tent.

"Chloe," a man's voice said as the figure drew nearer. "I've been waiting for you."

"You're my—you're Dante, aren't you?" Chloe whispered as the man's features became clearer.

He nodded. "We don't have much time. Hurry—you need to see something."

Chloe followed her great-grandfather past the tents, past a darkened stage and the bonfire to the other side of the clearing. And then suddenly there was nothing in front of them. No more ground, no more forest, no more starlit sky. It was as if they'd reached the edge of the world.

"Where are we?" Chloe said fearfully, taking a step back.

"Listen," Dante said, his hand on Chloe's arm. "You mustn't make the same mistake I made. Don't use the rose-wood box. Destroy it!"

"But—"

"Quickly," said Dante. "He's coming!"

Chloe looked over her shoulder and saw Mr. Dromnel and his beastly entourage entering the far side of the clearing. "Where do I go?" she cried, but Dante had disappeared. In desperation, Chloe tried to move forward, but it was like trying to swim through a thick cloud. She couldn't see anything in the empty space ahead, couldn't tell if she was making progress or just moving in place. Beneath the yelping and snarling coming from behind her, Chloe heard the faint ticking of a clock. The more she strained to push forward through the void, the louder it got. Vague shapes began to appear in front of her, as though she were looking at a scene through a gauze curtain. The shapes became clearer, resolving themselves into a scene that Chloe recognized. She was looking out at the dimly lit first-floor landing of her great-aunts' house. And then, as if an invisible curtain had fallen, the scene disappeared again.

"You're trapped," a voice whispered in her ear. Not Dante this time, but Mr. Dromnel.

"No," Chloe shuddered, but it was true. She was trapped in the painting on the landing, just like Dante and the others. With nowhere left to go, Chloe closed her eyes.

When Chloe opened her eyes again, she was back in her bed. She could feel her blankets and hear the rain, but the room seemed to be spinning, and she didn't know whether she was asleep or awake. After a moment her dizziness passed, and she was able to sit up. In the darkness, she saw that the closet door across the bedroom was ajar. A strange soft light spilled from its interior. Mesmerized, she rose from her bed and went to the source of the light. It was the rosewood box, glowing softly as if it had been painted with a phosphorescent stain. She picked it up and carried it to her bed. The lid fell back as she got under the covers, leaving the interior of the glowing box exposed and a faint sweet fragrance in the air.

"Look inside," said a smooth voice.

"I'm still dreaming," Chloe told herself, squeezing her eyes shut. "That's all it is, just a dream."

"Open your eyes, Chloe," said Mr. Dromnel's voice. "See what the box can give you."

Chloe's eyes remained closed, but she couldn't shut out the images that appeared on the inside of her eyelids. She saw herself standing on the dingy stage of her nightmare, paralyzed with fear, humiliated by her own insecurity. The scene changed. Now she stood in front of the cheering audience in the massive auditorium. They were giving her a standing ovation, crying out for an encore. Pride swelled her veins, radiated from every pore of her skin.

"Whisper your wish into the box and turn the key," said Mr. Dromnel.

"What will it cost me?" Chloe asked.

"What wouldn't you pay to win tomorrow? What wouldn't you sacrifice to keep winning all the way to a future of sold-out theaters and million-dollar recording contracts?"

Chloe felt the words forming on her tongue.

"That's right," Mr. Dromnel whispered. "It's the only thing that matters. The only thing you've ever wanted."

In her mind, Chloe could see his face. There was something new shining in his dark eyes, something like triumph. Then Mr. Dromnel's face dissolved. In its place she saw the beasts that had pursued her in her nightmare and Dante urging her to destroy the rosewood box.

"What will it cost me?" Chloe demanded again.

"There's always a price for greatness," said Mr. Dromnel. "There's very little room at the top. The winners in life are the ones who want victory the most, the ones willing to climb over everyone else to get there."

"No," said Chloe. She shook her head. "It doesn't have to be that way."

There was an edge of impatience in Mr. Dromnel's voice now. "Don't be naïve, Chloe. If you don't climb over them, they'll climb over you. Think about what you stand to gain—the money, the fame."

Once again Chloe found herself in the auditorium of her dream. Applause was pouring over her, lifting her up. But she felt strangely hollow this time, empty, as if something was missing. A final sequence of images flickered through her mind. Chloe saw Nyssa being flung from her bicycle, Nyssa lying in a hospital bed, her head bandaged, her arm in a cast. Chloe opened her eyes. "No," she said again with more conviction. "No!"

Her legs were over the side of the bed in an instant. With the rosewood box clutched in her hands, she ran from her bedroom, down the hall to the sitting room. The fire that had burned so brightly earlier that evening was still flickering as Chloe crossed to the hearth. She lifted the rosewood box and shoved it into the very center of the fire. Hungry tongues sprang to life around the dry wood. As the clock on the landing began to strike midnight, the rosewood box disappeared behind a curtain of dancing flames.

Chapter Fourteen

The storm had passed by the time Chloe opened her eyes the next morning. She let her eyelids fall shut again as she tried to make sense of the strange images and half-remembered dreams that still clouded her mind. "The box!" she said, leaping from her bed and running to the closet. Aside from a few pairs of shoes and a shirt that had fallen off its hanger, the closet floor was bare.

Chloe hurried down the hall to the sitting room. The fire was dead; only ash and charcoal remained in the stone fireplace. Chloe used a poker to dig through the charred debris. She found what she was looking for almost immediately: two hinges, a latch and a tiny key. She stared at the remains of the rosewood box; then she returned the poker to its hanger and stood up. There was one more thing she wanted to see.

A minute later, Chloe stood on the landing between the

first and second floors. "They're gone," she breathed, staring in wonder at the painting that hung on the wall beside the grandfather clock. What had once been a painting of Dante's carnival now displayed an empty meadow bordered by trees. The performers had disappeared. There was no trace of them. The tents, props and animals were gone as well.

Chloe ran her fingers lightly over the surface of the painting. It was dry, the pigment parched and cracking with age. She tried to lift the painting off the wall, but it wouldn't budge.

"I was afraid you weren't coming," Nyssa told Chloe a few hours later. "I'm sorry if I was a bully yesterday." Nyssa stood in front of St. Mark's Theater. She held one of the lobby doors ajar with the arm that wasn't in a cast. "I am glad you're here though."

Chloe was breathing hard as she followed Nyssa inside. "No worries—you were right. Sorry I'm late. Abigail's car battery died, and a neighbor tried to jump-start it but it didn't work, so I got a ride from the neighbor at the last minute instead. And there's so much more I have to tell you afterward!"

"They've just started," Nyssa said as they hurried across the empty lobby. "Are you nervous?"

Chloe nodded. "But I'm here."

"This is the easy part. It's just a tech rehearsal."

"Will I get a chance to play the piano before the show?" Chloe asked anxiously. "I need to get a feel for how the pedals and keys respond. Every piano is different."

"I'll check with my dad, but I think there's a sign-up sheet posted somewhere for people who want time on the stage this afternoon. I think everyone gets fifteen minutes. Is that enough?"

Chloe nodded. "That would be perfect."

"Here we go then," Nyssa said as she opened the door that led backstage. "Time to take your place in the lineup."

Chloe took a deep breath and followed her friend through the door.

Chloe was still forcing herself to take slow deep breaths as she made her way through the same door eight and a half hours later, this time without Nyssa at her side. Nyssa, Abigail, Bess and Kitty were all on their way into the theater to find their seats.

Chloe felt like a prisoner being led to the executioner's block as she followed the long concrete-lined hallway to a large dressing room. She was barely aware of the other young performers—her competition—already milling around as she entered the room. She found a folding chair and carried it over to an empty corner. With her eyes closed, she tried to visualize herself out on stage, lifting her fingers to play the first notes, playing her music smoothly and confidently from beginning to end.

"Are you all right?" someone asked.

Chloe opened her eyes and saw one of the festival organizers, a woman with long red hair tied back in a ponytail. "I'm fine," she said, forcing a smile.

The woman nodded sympathetically. "Last-minute jitters. Don't worry, you'll be fine once you're out there."

Chloe squeezed her eyes shut again and tried to return to her visualization exercise, but all she could see this time was the scene of her last humiliation. Her stomach gave a sudden heave. "Where's the washroom?" she asked a boy standing a few feet away. She made it to the toilet stall just in time.

A pale girl in black pants and a white blouse was standing at one of the sinks when Chloe emerged from the stall a few minutes later. She looked about Chloe's age. "Are you a first-timer too?" the girl asked.

"I've never been in this show, if that's what you mean. I've played at lots of recitals though," said Chloe. She turned on the faucet of the neighboring sink and cupped some water in her hands to rinse out her mouth.

The girl nodded. "My sister won second prize once in the dance category. She's in the Royal Winnipeg Ballet now."

Chloe dabbed at her face with a paper towel and straightened one of the clips that held her curls out of her face. "Well, good luck and all that," she said as she moved toward the door.

"I'm so scared," the girl said suddenly, her voice breaking.

Chloe turned and was surprised to see tears trickling down the girl's cheeks, leaving wet lines through the powdery foundation that covered her pale face. "You too?" said Chloe. "I just threw up. I'm terrified!"

"You are?"

"Completely," said Chloe.

"I'm Kimberly," the girl said as she wiped her tears away with a wadded piece of tissue.

"The cello player," said Chloe, remembering the name from the printed program. "You're on two people ahead of me."

Kimberly shook her head. Her long black ponytail swung behind her like a rope. "I can't go out on that stage tonight. There's no way."

"C'mon, you must have played at lots of recitals before."

"Never in front of an audience *this* size," Kimberly said, her voice taking on a desperate edge. "And there are TV cameras out there too. I can't do it. I just can't!"

Chloe felt her heart accelerate at the mention of the cameras. "So what are you going to do?"

"I'm going to hide out in one of the stalls. Don't tell them I'm in here, please!"

Chloe hesitated. "One less competitor," a voice in her head whispered. She took a deep breath and forced the thought out of her mind. She shook her head. "No way. If I'm going out there tonight, so are you. We can *do* this. C'mon, fix your makeup and let's get out of this bathroom."

The two girls stood together in the wings and watched their competitors performing on stage. Chloe felt her own anxiety ebb a little as she stood shoulder to shoulder with her new ally. She squeezed Kimberly's arm when the cellist's name was called.

"You can do it," Chloe whispered, repeating the words so many other people had used to encourage her. "Just keep breathing. Don't let yourself think about the audience until it's over. Don't think about the judges. Just think about the music. It's all about the music."

Although she had never heard Kimberly play before, Chloe sensed a little hesitation at the very beginning of her performance. After that, Kimberly seemed to get her bearings. She played the rest of the piece flawlessly, with just the right amount of emotion. Chloe clapped as proudly as any sister when Kimberly finished playing her second piece and came backstage to stand beside Chloe.

"Chloe McBride?" a man with a clipboard asked, causing her heart to leap back up in her throat. "You're up after the next kid. And here, I was asked to give you this."

It was a good-luck card, signed by Kitty, Bess, Nyssa and Abigail. Bess's short note caught Chloe off guard and brought her close to tears. *Trust yourself,* Chloe read, her hands trembling. *Whether you know it or not, you've spent half your life preparing for this moment. The music is inside you. Block everything else out and just focus on it. Let it out when you're ready. And no matter what happens on stage tonight, you can be proud just knowing that you were there when the curtain rose. By showing up tonight, you've proved that you are greater than your fears.*

"All right, it's your turn," said the man with the clipboard.

"Good luck," said Kimberly, her face shining.

Chloe felt herself being nudged on stage as the piano was rolled in from the other direction. The curtain went up, and suddenly there she was, standing in the spotlight at the front of a packed theater. It was too late to withdraw with any kind of dignity. For a second, Chloe remained frozen.

"Run," a voice in the back of her mind urged. *Not this time*, she told herself, standing her ground.

She bowed her head in acknowledgment of the welcoming applause and took her seat at the piano. After checking that her music was in place, she closed her eyes and took a few deep breaths. Her lips moved in silent prayer, and she opened her eyes again. She lifted her hands to the keys and began to play.

She knew after just a few bars that she was going to be okay. At the back of her mind she was aware of Nyssa and her aunts and Abigail sitting somewhere in the audience, watching her, praying for her, wishing her well. She felt the muscles in her arms relax, the tension in her chest slip away. She let go and fell into the music.

"You were *really* good," Kimberly said when Chloe was back in the wings again. "You're going to win something for sure."

Chloe let out a long breath and smiled. "I already did."

"You came *so* close to collecting the big prize tonight," said Nyssa. The two friends were seated on the steps of the veranda, Abigail's famous root-beer floats in their hands.

One of Chloe's curls sprang loose as she shook her head. "It wasn't close at all. That David Mu guy blew me away. I bet he got his first violin when he was, like, a month old."

"Yeah, well," Nyssa grinned, "second place isn't *too* bad, I guess."

"A miracle, really." Chloe shook her head again, this time in disbelief at the thought of what she'd just pulled off.

"You earned your award," Nyssa insisted. "There are no miracles."

"No miracles, huh? You *still* don't believe, even after what happened to the painting?"

"There's a rational explanation for everything," Nyssa said as she wiped some foam off her chin with the back of her hand. "There were multiple paintings and someone switched them on you. I've been saying that since the beginning."

"I told you, I tried to take it down this morning. You'd need a crowbar to get it off the wall. Besides, if there were multiple paintings, why didn't I find the rest of them when I searched the house?"

"Did you search your aunts' rooms? Or Abigail's?"

"All right then, Sherlock," said Chloe. "Since you seem to have an answer for everything, give me your explanation for Dante's disappearance."

Nyssa put her frosted glass down on the step. "Honestly? I think it was staged. Dante wanted to catch the world's attention by performing the greatest vanishing act of all time. Magdala might or might not have been in on it. I don't know."

"If it was staged, why didn't he ever come back?"

"Because the world didn't care whether he came back or not. They *still* weren't paying attention. Maybe he just lost it in the end."

"His family cared," Chloe insisted. "That should have been enough to bring him home."

There was sympathy in Nyssa's eyes as she faced her friend. "Sometimes people who disappear don't know how to come back again. Even famous magicians."

"Maybe," Chloe said. "But in a strange way I think he did come back for a little while this summer."

The two friends fell silent as the sun set over the canal.

"Who knows," Nyssa said at last, pushing herself up from the step. "Maybe you're right."

"Thanks, Nyssa" said Chloe. "And thank you too, Dante, wherever you are."

Acknowledgments

I am grateful to Sarah Wood for sharing her insight as a performer and pianist. Thanks also to my husband, Bernard, and my daughters, Rebecca, Naomi and Emily, for their endless confidence and support. A special thank-you to Sarah Harvey, my editor, who led me with patience and much kind encouragement to the heart of Chloe's story.

Rachel Dunstan Muller was born in California and immigrated to Canada as a young child. With the exception of a year in Northern Ireland, she has lived on the west coast of British Columbia since the age of ten. She has been an English tutor, a ferry worker, a newspaper columnist and a training consultant, but writing fiction is her favorite occupation. Rachel currently lives in a small Vancouver Island community with her husband, four children, and an ever-changing assortment of cats, rabbits, birds, rodents, amphibians and fish.

Recent award-winning books from Orca Book Publishers

Summer on the Run
Nancy Belgue

The Bone Flute
Patricia Bow

The Puppet Wrangler
Vicki Grant

Quid Pro Quo
Vicki Grant

Safe House
James Heneghan

The Mask on the Cruise Ship
Melanie Jackson

Dog House Blues
Jacqueline Pearce

The Truth About Rats (and Dogs)
Jacqueline Pearce

For more information on these titles and all of Orca's books, please visit www.orcabook.com